THE NEW WINDMILL BOOK OF
HAUNTING TALES

EDITED BY ROBERT ETTY

Heinemann
New Windmills

Heinemann Educational Publishers
Halley Court, Jordan Hill, Oxford OX2 8EJ
a division of Reed Educational & Professional Publishing Ltd

MELBOURNE   AUCKLAND
FLORENCE   PRAGUE   MADRID   ATHENS
SINGAPORE   TOKYO   SAO PAULO
PORTSMOUTH NH   MEXICO CITY
IBADAN   GABORONE   JOHANNESBURG
KAMPALA   NAIROBI

2001 2000 99 98 97
10 9 8 7 6 5 4 3 2

ISBN 0 435 12478 1

Acknowledgements
The editor and publisher wish to acknowledge the assistance of Mrs Pat Salton and the staff of
Louth Library, Lincolnshire, and should like to thank the following for permission to use
copyright material:
Scholastic Publications Ltd for 'Snapdragon' by Gillian Cross © Gillian Cross, from *Chilling
Christmas Tales*, published by Scholastic, 1992, p1; Jennifer Luithlen for 'A Lot of Mince Pies'
by Robert Swindells © Robert Swindells, from *The Oxford Book of Christmas Stories* published
by OUP, 1986, p20; John Murray Publishers Ltd for 'The Lost Boy' by George Mackay Brown
from *Andrina and Other Stories*, p20; copyright © Jean Richardson 1985, for her story 'Not at
Home' from *Cold Feet*, published by Hodder & Stoughton, p35; David Higham Associates for
'Rummins' from *Someone Like You* by Roald Dahl, published by Penguin, p48; A P Watt Ltd on
behalf of John Gordon for 'Left in the Dark' by John Gordon from *Ghost Stories*, edited by
Robert Westall published by Kingfisher, 1991, p63; Faber and Faber Ltd for 'The Deadfall' from
Difficulties of a Bridegroom, Collected Short Stories by Ted Hughes, published by Faber and
Faber Ltd, p91; Heinemann Publishers for 'The Guitarist' by Grace Hallworth from *Mouth Open,
Story Jump Out*, published by Methuen, 1984, p114; Jennifer Luithlen Agency for 'The Servant'
by Alison Prince © Alison Prince from *The Green Ghost and Other Ghost Stores* ed. Mary
Danby, published by HarperCollins, p117; Penguin Books for 'The Call' from *The Call and Other
Stories* by Robert Westall © Robert Westall, published by Viking, 1989, p134.
Every effort has been made to contact copyright holders. We should be glad to rectify any
omissions at the next reprint if notice is given to the publisher.

Cover illustration by Brian Lee
Cover design by The Point
Typeset by Books Unlimited (Nottm) NG19 7QZ
Printed and bound in the United Kingdom by Clays Ltd, St Ives plc

Contents

Introduction

Haunting tales catch us unawares and refuse to let us go. They lead us to unlikely places and show us amazing things. They make us see shadows, hear footsteps and bristle with fear. Then, long after we first met them, they slip back into our minds, restored to life by something someone says, a picture, somewhere we visit – or simply when we are alone and allow our imaginations to wander.

In this collection are stories by some of our most acclaimed authors. They tell of country ghosts and town ghosts; of mysterious events in sunlight and starlight, on hot mornings and snowy nights; of foxes and rats; of candles and campfires; of strange whispers and telephone calls; of a summer bike-ride into the past and the horror endured by a carol singer one frosty Christmas Eve.

Enjoy the stories now – and perhaps, some day when you do not expect it, one of them will return to haunt you!

Robert Etty

Snapdragon
Gillian Cross

The tiny lights sparkled, reflected in all directions, as Tod and Ben slouched round the corner. Ben saw them twinkle like stars, through the tall, feathery leaves of the pot plant that Tod had just bought for his mother. Red and yellow and green stars. Bright pinpoints, scattered from top to bottom of the Christmas tree in the big bay window.

Three children crowded round the tree, staring at the lights and pointing at the little parcels hidden among the branches. Their mother reached over their heads to drape on the last strands of tinsel, and their father stood on a ladder, holding the star that was going on the very top.

The perfect Christmas Eve picture.

'*Ah*!' said Tod, sarcastically. 'How *sweet*! Just hold this a moment, will you?'

Carelessly, he pushed the pot plant into Ben's hands, not even noticing that he was bending one of the leaves. His eyes were fixed on the bright Christmas window, and there was an angry flare to his nostrils.

Ben knew that look. It always meant trouble. But he couldn't escape, because he had taken the plant from Tod. 'I don't think –' he began.

Tod ignored him. 'Get behind the hedge. And keep your mouth shut.'

Ben ducked down on the other side of the hedge and watched through a gap as Tod crept towards the door and reached for the bellpush.

DRRRRRRRRRRR!

An electric bell rang inside the house and Tod shot out of the garden and flung himself down beside Ben. His eyes were glittering and he was breathing fast as he watched the picture in the window splinter. The children turned away from the tree, and their mother disappeared.

A second later she flung open the door, with a smile that dissolved when she saw no one there. She looked briefly up and down the road, tossed her head and slammed the door. When she walked back into the sitting room, she pulled the curtains briskly.

'Stupid cow!' Tod said, with satisfaction. 'Come on.'

He sauntered away up the road, leaving Ben to trail behind with the plant. The broken leaf had snapped off, and Ben looked down to flick it on to the pavement. When he looked up, he saw that Tod had stopped again.

He was staring up at a first floor window. In the dim light of a bedside lamp, a little boy sat up in his bunk, watching his father fix a stocking to the end of the bed. He was chewing his teddy's ear, and his eyes were open very wide.

'Getting ready for Santa!' Tod spat into the gutter as Ben came up beside him. 'Let's give them a bit of excitement while they're waiting.'

He was at the front door while Ben was still thinking where to hide. Jamming his finger defiantly on the bell-push, he grinned over his shoulder as Ben scrambled into the shelter of the wall next door. Then, when the door began to open, he took two steps sideways, into the shadow of a big holly bush.

The little boy's father opened the door and his face twisted.

'Louts!' he yelled, into the dark garden. 'Haven't you got anything better to do?'

Behind him, Ben saw the little boy drag his teddy to the top of the stairs.

'Daddy!' he whined. 'You said we were going to do my stocking –'

The door shut, sharply, and Tod strolled out of his hiding place, looking pleased with himself.

'Where shall we go now?'

Ben shifted the plant pot to his other arm, catching it on the wall by mistake. 'I can't hang around, Tod. Honest. I've got to get home. With it being Christmas Eve.'

Tod's grin hardened. 'Got to get back to your mummy? Your darling daddy will be worrying, will he? Go on then. Don't let me stop you.' He wrenched the plant roughly out of Ben's hands.

'You don't have to –' Ben said, uneasily. 'I mean, why don't you come too? Mum won't mind.'

Tod didn't say anything. Just stood there, looking, waiting for Ben to crack.

Ben put his hands into his pockets, hesitating. 'What time does your mum get in, then?'

'How should I know? Midnight? One o'clock? She's not going to stay stuck in on her own, with me, is she? With it being Christmas Eve.'

Tod started to walk off up the road, elaborately slowly, not bothering to look back at Ben, who was trailing a foot or two behind.

'OK,' Ben said, crossly. 'I'll hang around for a bit. If you like. What are we going to do?'

'Dunno.' Tod looked up and down the road. 'How about –' Suddenly, he grinned. 'Hey, let's knock the grey house.'

He pointed ahead, at the big corner house that sprawled ahead of them. Its front was dark and hidden, shrouded by the overgrown bushes in the garden. But the low side fence let them see the bare wall that stretched back from the pavement.

'That's dumb. No one lives there. Only –' Ben's eyes flickered away from it.

'Only *ghosts*?' Tod looked tauntingly at him. 'Oh, come *on*, Benno. We're not little kids any more. Anyway, what d'you call that?'

He pointed to the small window at the back of the side wall. Its curtains were half open and faintly, in the gap between them, Ben glimpsed a flickering blue light.

'How should I know what it is?'

'Gho-o-osts!' Tod said again, opening his eyes wide.

'Do us a favour!' Ben was trying to sound tough, but his voice snagged in his throat, and Tod whooped with triumph.

'They're watching telly, saphead! Come on.'

Grabbing Ben's hand, he dragged him along the pavement to the front gate. The path to the house was long and dark, almost closed in by the overgrown bushes. Ben could hardly make out the front door at the far end.

'Scared?' Tod said, needling him.

'Oh yes! Sure!' said Ben.

But he couldn't get the right, sarcastic note in his

voice and Tod was grinning as he unlatched the gate. 'After you, ghostbuster.'

Ben took a step into the garden. There was barely room to walk between the bushes. Their twigs caught at his clothes, and the leafless branches rustled dryly. Under his feet, the tiled path was slippery with old, wet moss.

But he couldn't back out. Tod was right behind him, so close that the tattered leaves of the pot plant were brushing his neck. Uneasily, he began to walk forwards, placing his feet very carefully so that he would not fall. He tried not to notice how the bushes closed him in, shutting out everything beyond the path except for the solid, dark shape of the front door.

They were there too soon. Ben stopped dead when he reached the stone steps that led up to the door. Leaning forwards, Tod whispered in his ear.

'Go on, then. Ring it.'

'Me?' Ben swallowed.

'It's your turn, Benny-boy. I don't want to hog all the fun.'

Tod's face was hidden in the shadows, but Ben could *hear* the taunting smile on it. Slowly he ran a finger over the cracked, splintering paint, and a flake broke off and caught under his fingernail. Then he reached up, and tugged at the bell-pull.

The silence exploded into a loud jangle of brass, just on the other side of the door. Ben snatched his hand away, but that didn't stop the noise. The bell was swinging wildly, and the noise went on. And on and on and on.

Pushing past Tod, Ben turned and ran for the gate. His breath caught in his throat and by the time he reached the pavement he was sweating. He didn't realize that Tod was not following until he heard his voice, swearing softly from the shadows.

'That's right! Save your own skin. What about me? Just going to leave me here to rot, are you?'

Ben put his head back into the tunnel of bushes. 'Stop fooling about! Get out of there!'

'Yes *sir*! Just wait while I leap to my feet –'

The words were cut off short as Tod caught his breath. Even from the other end of the tunnel, Ben heard it quite plainly. He pushed the gate open and stepped back into the garden.

'If you're trying to trick me –'

'Think I'm daft?' Tod said bitterly. 'I tripped over the bootscraper. Think I've broken my –'

He caught his breath again, and Ben crept back up the path, watching the front door all the time. Tod was slumped on the steps, with his head against the door frame. Ben grabbed his shoulders and tried to drag him to his feet, but Tod lashed out sideways with the pot, knocking Ben's hands away.

'Don't do that!'

'But you've got to get up. How are you going to walk?'

'I can't walk!' Tod snapped. 'Unless you want me to be sick all over your shoes. You try knocking your ankle to bits.'

Ben looked down helplessly. 'Well – how about crawling?'

'Oh, wonderful! All the way home?'

Ben could imagine his sour, scornful expression. 'What are you going to do, then?'

Tod wriggled round and grabbed at Ben's anorak.

'*I'm* not going to do anything except go on lying here. But *you're* going to ring that bell again. And ask if they'll let you phone your darling daddy. I'll never get home unless someone brings a car for me.'

'But no one came the last time I rang.' Ben looked nervously at the bell-pull. 'Maybe they won't –'

Tod's fingers twisted the corner of the anorak into a rope. '*Make* them come. We know there's someone there, because we saw the television light.'

'But –'

'Go *on!*'

Ben grabbed the big brass knocker in the centre of the door, meaning to hammer as hard as he could. But as soon as he touched it, the door swung away from him, into the house. He was looking down a dark, narrow hall, with closed doors on either side.

'H-hallo?' he stammered. 'Is there anyone there?'

No one answered, but he caught a glimpse of something like movement at the far end of the hall. The last door on the left was not quite shut, and cold blue light flickered in the opening. Raising his voice, Ben called again.

'Hallo?'

From behind the open door came a faint, cracked voice. 'Down here.'

Ben looked sideways at Tod, waiting for some clue about what to do. But it was till too dark to see his face. And anyway, he could guess what Tod would say.

He walked up the two stone steps and into the hall. Chill, damp air closed round him, lying against his cheeks and seeping up his nose. It seemed heavier than any air he had ever breathed before. He stopped for a second.

7

'What's the matter with you?' Tod dragged himself upright, clinging to the door frame with one hand and swinging the pot plant in the other. He hauled himself up the steps and then lurched sideways, to fling an arm round Ben's neck. 'Get a move on! I'll come with you – if you're *scared*.'

Ben wanted to push him away, to insist on going on his own. But the cold air choked back the words and he let Tod's arm stay where it was. Slowly, without speaking, the two of them began to move down the hall.

The floor was made of stone tiles, and Tod's foot slapped down heavily each time he hopped, but no one came out to see what the noise was. Step by step, pausing every now and then for Tod to catch his breath, they drew nearer to the half-open door.

When they reached it, Tod transferred his weight to the wall and waved his free hand. 'After you, sir.'

'Hallo?' Ben said for the third time. He cleared his throat noisily and looked at the light that danced against the wall in front of him. *Television,* Tod had said. But it wasn't. It was too blue for that.

On the other side of the door, there was a faint sound, like feet moving on a carpet. 'Come in,' said the cracked, old voice.

Ben pushed at the door and it swung away from him. For a second, he glimpsed the dark shapes of scattered chairs. Then the door opened wider, and he couldn't look at anything except the long table in the middle of the room.

And the fire.

There was a wide, shallow dish in the centre of the table, and it was full of blue fire, burning in a shallow, luminous layer. The flames wriggled and flickered from side to side, like live creatures, constantly moving, and the shadows of the room moved with them, swaying and twisting grotesquely.

The figure crouched over the fire was moving as well. She stood with her back to them, stooped forward so that her ragged hair swung round her face. And her small, stiff body jerked, like the body of a bird. Forward. Back. Forward again. Her hand snatched at the fire, sharp and quick as a pecking beak.

'Please –' Ben said uncertainly.

She stopped, with her hand halfway to the fire, but she didn't turn. Only her head tilted slightly, waiting for what was coming.

'We need to use your phone,' Tod said. 'I can't –'

'No phone!'

Suddenly, startlingly, she laughed, snatching at the fire again and then whirling round, with her hands stretched out towards them.

Fire danced on her fingertips.

They burned blue, licked by little flames that snaked towards the first joint and then shrank back again. The light distorted her smile, making her nose sharp and bright-pointed, and plunging her eyes into deep shadow.

Tod grabbed at Ben's shoulder. 'What the –'

The old woman waved her hands at them and laughed again, baring her teeth. The blue light danced on stained fangs, scattered survivors in a mouthful of empty spaces.

'Coming to play?' she hissed. 'Or are you scared?'

'Can't see anything to be scared of.'

Tod said it defiantly, but his voice was too loud and the laugh came again, like the wind in dead leaves. 'Come and play Snapdragon!'

The old woman waved her hands at them and laughed again, baring her teeth

She beckoned them slowly, with a shrunken hand that suddenly darted away, into the centre of the fire. Ben saw her snatch up something and cram it into her mouth.

'Let's get out of here,' he muttered.

'Are you crazy?' Tod was staring at the blue fire. His tongue flicked quickly over his top lip. 'I'm going to play.'

He grabbed at Ben's shoulder and forced him forward, hopping just behind. Together, they lurched towards the table, Tod's foot thudding on the thin carpet. As soon as they were near enough, he seized a chair and flopped down into it, dumping the remains of his mother's plant on the table.

'Now!' he said. His tongue flicked again, catching the corner of his mouth, and Ben heard him breathing, shallow and fast.

'Tod!' he hissed. 'Don't –'

But Tod's hand was already hovering over the fire, wavering uncertainly as he peered into it.

The old woman tipped her head sideways, her mouth twisting into a mocking smile – and Tod grabbed.

His hand came out flaming blue at the fingertips, and Ben gasped, before he could stop himself.

'Tod –'

'Don't be soft!' Tod snapped. 'It doesn't hurt.' He pushed something into his mouth and grinned up at the old woman.

'Almonds!'

She laughed her thin, rustling laugh. 'Sweet or bitter?'

'They're good.' Tod nudged Ben. 'Come on. Try it.' He dipped into the tray again, feeling round greedily, and then snatched his hand away and swore.

The old woman tittered in the shadows. 'Be *quick*!' Her hand darted in and out, and Ben heard the almond crunch between her ruined teeth.

The flames were beginning to die, dwindling and shrinking in towards the middle of the tray. As they grew smaller, Ben stretched his hand out, trying to pluck up courage to plunge in.

'Do it like this!' Tod snatched again, laughing as he waved a flaming raisin under Ben's nose.

'Like this!' The old woman grabbed a fistful of almonds and tipped them in a burning stream from one hand to the other.

'Before it's too late!' Tod pushed Ben's hand down towards the last patch of blue, but Ben pulled it back automatically, shrinking away from the fire.

And then he'd missed it.

The last little flames ran along one side of the tray and dwindled into tiny, formless blobs. Then they went out, and the room was dark.

The old woman gave a long sigh. 'Turn on the light.'

'The–?' Ben looked stupidly at the tray, and she stamped her foot.

'By the door!'

Picking his way across the room, Ben fumbled round the door frame and flicked the switch. He didn't realize how frightened he had been until the shadows dissolved – and left him standing in an ordinary, shabby dining room. The flat brightness of electric light lit up worn chairs and stained wallpaper, without any sign of Christmas to brighten the drabness. No tinsel, no decorations, not even a Christmas card.

The only unusual thing was the old tin tray on the table. Nuts and raisins were scattered all over it and round them was a trickle of dark brown liquid.

Tod dipped a finger into it and tasted it. 'Brandy?'

The old woman chuckled. 'I had half a bottle in there.'

The words sounded comfortable and ordinary and, in the light, she was ordinary too. Small and shrivelled, with a bony nose and liver-spotted hands. The only strange thing about her was the blue bow in her straggling white hair.

Ben was so relieved that he almost laughed. '*Brandy?*'

'Of course,' she said gravely. 'We always had a snapdragon on Christmas Eve. Everyone played it in those days, and we were crazy about it. Mother had to fight to save enough brandy for the pudding. The boys always tried to wheedle some more. *Give us another go, Ma! The pudding won't need all that!* She got so cross with them!' The dry old voice creaked into laughter and she stroked the rim of the tray with one finger.

Just an old-fashioned Christmas game! Ben turned to grin at Tod, to share the joke.

But Tod wasn't watching him. He was staring admiringly at the old woman. 'I bet it wasn't just the boys she got cross with. I bet you nagged her worse than they did. You're so good at it. Much better than I am.'

She flicked the rim of the tray, so that it rang like a bell. And when she spoke again, her voice was cold. 'Oh, they never let me play. I was too young.' For a moment she looked sulky, like a bad-tempered child.

'Make up for it now, then.' Tod put his elbows on the table. 'Let's have another game.'

'I really ought to go –' Ben said, reluctantly, but Tod snorted.

'Don't be so *wet*. You haven't even tried it yet. I think we ought to have another game.'

'You do?' The old woman looked steadily at Tod for a moment, and Ben suddenly noticed how blue her eyes were. A clear, startling blue, as bright as her ribbon.

'Why not?' Tod said. 'Have you got any more brandy?'

'It's in the kitchen.' The blue eyes suddenly swivelled round to Ben. 'You can go and get it if you like. Across the hall.'

Ben shuffled his feet. 'Really – my mum and dad are expecting me – I promised –'

'Such a *good* little boy!' Tod rolled his eyes up at the ceiling. 'Why don't you set the snapdragon burning first? Then you can leave me here while you go and get your dad.'

The old woman smiled at Ben, tilting her head on one side. 'You can use all the rest of the brandy. Put it in the saucepan to warm –'

'I know how to do it,' muttered Ben. 'I've watched Dad, when he does it for the pudding.'

'Aren't you the lucky one,' Tod said sourly. 'With a darling daddy who's around at Christmas. And a precious mummy who bothers with Christmas puddings.' He flicked the tin tray with his fingernail, as the old woman had done, and then dropped his head, listening as it rang.

Ben walked across the hall, found the kitchen and switched on the light. There was grease on the rickety old table and the sink was cracked, but he saw the brandy bottle straight away. It stood by the cooker, with a small saucepan and a box of matches next to it. Unscrewing the top, he poured all the brandy into the saucepan.

The gas seemed to take a long time to come through, and the first match burnt right down to his fingers. But at last the flame came, with a vigorous pop, and he stood the saucepan over it. As the brandy began to warm, he caught the familiar, mixed, once-a-year smells of brandy and gas and burnt matches.

And he wanted to be at home.

His mother would be in the kitchen, swigging sherry and making mince pies. And Dad would be teasing Mary and Laura, pretending that he couldn't find the stockings. What was he doing in this cold, dark house, with no one but Tod and a stranger?

Lighting another match, Ben held it over the saucepan until the brandy caught fire with a small, soft explosion. Then he walked across the hall, calling as he went.

'Coming! Are you ready?'

The old woman flicked the light off as he went into the dining room and he carried the panful of blue flames over to the table.

'Here we go, then. Happy Christmas!'

He poured out the brandy in a steady, glowing stream, until the tray was a sea of fire again. Then he swung the saucepan away.

'OK. I'm off.'

But he hesitated for a second, waiting to be persuaded out of it. Waiting for Tod to say, *Stay a bit* or *Have a turn before you go*.

Only Tod wasn't thinking about him at all. He just flapped a vague hand in Ben's direction and muttered, 'Great. See you in a minute.' His eyes were on the flames, and his hand was already hovering over the tray, ready to pounce.

But the old woman beat him to it. Her hand dived forward, into the very centre of the flames.

'A raisin!'

'Don't pinch them all!' Tod grabbed too, and grinned at her as he pushed two almonds into his mouth.

For a second, Ben watched them. Then he walked out of the room and down the dark hall. As he pulled the front door shut behind him, he could see the orange brightness of street lights at the other end of the tunnel of bushes, and he heard the church clock strike seven. Mary and Laura's bedtime.

He started to run, but he didn't get far. Halfway up the hill, a car slid along the pavement and drew up beside him, and his father leaned over to open the passenger door.

'Where have you been? The girls are ready to hang up their stockings, and you promised you'd be back to do yours at the same time.'

'I was just coming. But Tod –'

'Groan!' His father pulled a face. 'Couldn't he spare you for once? It *is* Christmas.'

'He's hurt his ankle,' Ben said. 'Maybe even broken it.' He slid into the car and pulled the door shut. 'We'll have to give him a lift home, Dad.'

His father gave another dramatic groan. 'No use taking him home. I don't suppose that mother of his will be around to look after him. We'd better get him straight to Casualty. Where is he?'

'In the grey house.' Ben pointed.

His father looked sharply at him. 'Have you been breaking in?'

'Of course not! The old lady asked us to go in.'

'Old lady?'

'She's living there now.'

There was another sharp look, but his father didn't say anything. He just turned left at the bottom of the hill and pulled up outside the grey house.

Ben was out of the car while the engine was still running. 'I'll get him.'

The path between the bushes was still dark, but this time his father was watching from beyond the gate. Ben strode up to the door and tugged hard at the bell-pull.

He knew he would have to wait. Tod couldn't get to the door and it would take the old woman some time to walk down the hall. Ben stood with his arms folded, listening for the sound of feet.

But no one came.

The car door slammed, and his father walked up the path. 'Having problems?'

'No one's answering.' Ben frowned. 'They *must* be able to hear –'

His father was examining the door, tapping at the top and the bottom of it. 'This feels as though it's boarded up on the inside.'

'But that's impossible! We went in –' Ben swallowed, and stopped.

'I'm going round the back,' his father said, abruptly. 'I'll see if I can get in that way.'

He dived off to the right, pushing his way through the bushes, and Ben stood looking after him for a moment. Then he remembered the side window. He struggled the other way through the bushes and ran down the side path.

He could see the little window ahead of him, with its curtains still half open and the gap lit by that blue glow that Tod had mistaken for the light from a television. Heading straight for it, he ploughed across a flower bed and pressed his nose to the glass.

And there they were. Two figures, facing each other across the blazing snapdragon. Tod was grinning and laughing out loud as his hands dipped into the tray and came out flaming bright. He tossed the nuts and raisins into the air, catching them between his teeth and gazing tauntingly over the table as he chewed them with his mouth open.

The person on the other side of the table laughed back at him, her perfect white teeth gleaming in the blue light. She had pushed her brown curls back over her shoulder and they bounced on the lacy collar of her velvet dress as she bobbed forward towards the tray.

Beyond, the feathery plant spread its leaves like a tiny, moonlit tree, every delicate, beautiful frond dancing as the flames danced. Light winked back from gleaming, polished wood and bright festoons of tinsel. Glasses twinkled on a sideboard where bottles stood shoulder to shoulder, and a plateful of mince pies lay next to a big, iced cake. Every inch of the room was warm and glittering and full of Christmas.

For a second, Ben was hollow with longing to be there, to be part of that perfect Christmas Eve picture. But he knew it was too late. He couldn't get back now.

Raising his hand, he knocked on the window.

The girl whirled round to face him, and he had one glimpse of her unmistakable blue eyes. Blue as the ribbon that tied up her curls. Then the last flame on the tray flickered and shrank to nothing, and the snapdragon went out.

At the same moment, there was a sound of splintering wood as the back door gave way. Then heavy footsteps echoed from the tiled hall and his father called out to him.

'It's like I said, Ben. There's nobody here. Nobody at all.'

A Lot of Mince Pies
Robert Swindells

I wish to God I'd never heard of the school choir, and I'm not the only one. In three days' time we'll go carolling round the village, same as every year. We'll work our melodious way along the high-street, trekking up gravel driveways to do our stuff and knock for donations. All proceeds to local charities. We'll do all the posh houses on Micklebarrow Close, then the Red Lion and the supermarket car-park. The supermarket'll be open late and seething with last-minute shoppers as it always is on Christmas Eve. We never fail to make a killing there. And after that we'll move out to where the street-lamps end and do some of the cottages and a farm or two. The cottages are a dead loss as far as money's concerned, but school choirs have sung outside them since just after the dinosaurs and we carry on the tradition. The farms are better. They know we're coming so they keep the dogs in and do hot mince pies and ginger wine for us. I can't stand mince pies.

Anyway, from the minute we troop out of the school-yard behind old Exley at seven o'clock, the kids'll be waiting for one thing. They'll be waiting for the last house – the Meltons' place, with its tangled garden, crumbling brick, and funny little windows. It's three-quarters of a mile from the village, and the choir usually gets there about nine o'clock. The Meltons'll be waiting, and as soon as we strike up the first number they'll open the door and stand there in carpet-slippers, smiling and swaying a little to the music. They're the most ancient couple you're ever likely to see – my mum says they were old when she was in the choir – but the thing about them is, you can actually see that they're enjoying the carols, and afterwards they make a generous donation and give presents to all the kids. There's always eighteen in the choir and I suppose the Meltons buy the stuff on their Christmas shopping expedition, but I don't know where they go – nobody ever sees them in the village. The presents aren't tatty either – none of your quid-a-dozen made in Taiwan plastic rubbish. They tend to be things like cartridge pens, penknives and wallets and purses made of real leather. Last year I got a calculator. As soon as the singing's over they beckon some kid inside – someone whose face they've taken a fancy to, I suppose – and the chosen one reappears a few minutes later with a double armful of little packets.

By now you'll be thinking this sounds like the perfect end to Christmas Eve and wondering why I'm moaning. Hang about, and I'll tell you what happened last year.

It was a clear, starry night, and the hoar-frost was already forming on the grass as we left the last of the farms behind and set off to sing for the Meltons. The fields were sheets of silver and the hedges were black and I slackened my pace till a gap opened between me and the others. It was very still and quiet, and suddenly I got this feeling that once, on a frosty night long ago, somebody like me had passed this way alone. I don't know what brought it on but it was a heck of a strong feeling – like being haunted without actually seeing anything. I shivered, and then a wave of sadness hit me for that unknown walker, long since dead. It must have been the quiet that did it – that or the moonlight. Anyway it rattled me, and I was glad when Shaun Wrigley noticed I wasn't with the party and turned, shouting to me to get a move on.

We got to the Meltons' place at ten past nine. One downstairs window strained pale light through its curtain but the garden was black. The gate had no top hinge and old Exley had to lift it before he could open it. It squealed, and when he dropped it there were glove-prints in its coating of frost.

Beyond the gate, some sunflowers had blown over. Their dried-out heads hung low across the path. They nodded and crackled as we waded through them. One snapped off and Shaun Wrigley booted it. It cart-wheeled up the path shedding seeds, then veered off into long grass. We formed an arc around the door, shuffling and clearing our throats. Our breath hung in clouds round our heads.

'Right, folks?' old Exley whispered. He only called us folks on Christmas Eve. '"Hark the Herald", after two.' He counted us in and we were away.

They must have been waiting behind the door, because halfway through line three the latch clicked and it swung inwards and there they were, him with his arm round her shoulder, nodding in time with the music. You couldn't tell if they were smiling because what light there was was behind them, but you got the impression that they were.

We formed an arc around the door, shuffling and clearing our throats

We went through our repertoire, making a pretty good job of it. My feet got so cold standing still I couldn't feel them, but I didn't mind. It was our last stint, and in ten minutes or so I'd be on my way home with the job behind me for another year and a nice little gift in my pocket.

Our last number was 'We Wish You a Merry Christmas'. Nobody could accuse us of originality. As the final note died away, the Meltons clapped. They always did that. The old guy flapped a hand and said, 'Let that one come in – the one with the bobble-cap.' We were all bunched together so you couldn't tell who he meant, and I'd forgotten I had my pom-pom hat on so I didn't move. Old Exley craned over the kids' heads, trying to see where old Melton was pointing. He spotted my pom-pom and said, 'Wake up, lad – the gentleman's waiting.'

I hurried forward, feeling myself go red. As I did so this third-year girl, Stephanie Williams, said something I didn't catch and made a half-hearted grab for my sleeve. She had a funny look on her face but she's a peculiar girl at the best of times and I just sort of jerked my arm out of her reach and brushed past. It wasn't till I was inside with my hat in my hand that I remembered Stephanie'd been the chosen one last year.

I was standing in a stone-flagged passageway. To my left a door stood ajar. Light trickled feebly from beyond it, falling in a wedge across the flags. I saw slug-trails and there was a flat, fungoid smell.

The old woman slipped a hand under my elbow and began steering me along the passageway. Beyond the puddle of light I was virtually blind. Behind me, the old man closed the door.

'This way, my dear.' The woman guided me to the foot of some wooden stairs that went up into blackness. I didn't want to insult them or hurt their feelings or anything, but the creepiness of the place was getting to me and I hung back a bit. 'Is there a light?' I ventured.

'Oh, no, dear.' She sounded surprised – shocked, almost. The old man, shuffling after us, said, 'He can't do with the light, you see.'

'Who?' My scalp prickled. We began climbing the uncarpeted stairs.

'Why, Gilbert of course,' said the woman. 'Our little son. He can't do with it, can he, Daddy?'

'No, Mummy,' her husband replied. 'He's a good boy, but he can't do with the light at all.'

As we ascended the air grew colder and the rank smell more intrusive. The woman's fingers felt like claws in the crook of my elbow, and suddenly I wanted to break free and run for it. I didn't, because the man was right behind us and because I didn't fancy looking like a wally in front of the choir. Instead I said, 'I didn't know you had a boy.' My voice sounded shaky, even to me.

'Oh, yes,' crooned the woman. 'We've had him ever such a long time haven't we, Daddy?'

'A long, long time, Mummy,' old Melton confirmed, and it occurred to me that they were probably mad. It was Christmas Eve and here I was in the dark with a pair of decrepit lunatics who thought they had a kid called Gilbert.

At the top of the stairs was a creaky landing. It was not completely dark, because there was a door with about an inch of bluish light showing under it. Mrs Melton let go my arm and whispered, 'Gilbert's room.

I'll open the door, and you can pop in and give him his present.'

'Present?' A mixture of dread and embarrassment scrambled my brain. I had no present. Was I supposed to have? Perhaps a gift for Gilbert was part of the yearly ritual. If so, nobody'd told me. I flushed in the chill gloom, stammering, 'I – I'm sorry, Mrs Melton. I didn't know. I haven't –'

'Yes, you have.' I started as the old man, who must have crept up behind me, hissed in my ear. His breath smelled vile.

The only thing I had was my hat, now a damp, screwed-up lump in my hands. I remembered he'd mentioned it outside. The one with the bobble cap. Stupidly, I held it out. 'This – you mean this?' He chuckled.

'A kiss,' he whispered. 'Only a kiss, under the mistletoe.'

'I'm a boy,' I croaked, appalled. 'I don't kiss other boys.'

He didn't reply.

The woman stretched up and drew a bolt near the top of the door. It grated and slammed. As the echo died I heard something else – an uncouth, wordless cry from the room beyond, and I knew then that Gilbert was real and that there must be something horribly wrong with him. She bent and drew a second bolt.

I don't know why I didn't turn then and run. I'll never know. I only know I've spent every day since wishing I had.

The door swung inward.

'Gilbert,' the woman crooned. 'Here's somebody with a present for you, darling.' I couldn't see past her.

The old man laid an arm across my shoulders and pushed me forward. I was half resisting and he really had to exert pressure. He kept murmuring, 'Come along – come along,' as though he was talking to a stubborn infant. If I'd dug my heels in he wouldn't have stood a chance, but even now a part of me was scared of hurting their feelings. A mistletoe kiss seems such a small thing, and how do you tell parents nicely that the thought of being in the same room with their kid makes you want to throw up, let alone kissing him?

The woman moved aside. There was a bed. Above the bed a dim blue lightbulb burned. Somebody had fastened a sprig of mistletoe to its dusty, fraying flex. The light fell on rumpled sheets, and on the boy they called Gilbert.

I gaped. God knows what I'd been expecting – some slavering, semi-human monster I suppose, but Gilbert was beautiful. I know it's a funny word to use about a boy but he was. He lay, propped on one elbow, looking at me through dark, liquid, lemur's eyes. His tip-tilted nose cast a smudge of shadow across a mobile mouth. His hair fell in a dark cascade to his shoulders, concealing the hand that supported his head. His frame was lean, his pale skin smooth as cream.

Old Melton dropped his hand to the small of my back and pushed gently. 'Go on now, boy – one little kiss, that's all.'

I moved towards the bed, but it wasn't the old man's hand that made me. It was partly relief of course – relief that I wasn't about to touch some unspeakable horror with my lips, but mostly it was Gilbert's eyes. I read a bit once out of a book my mum was reading. It was a romance, and somebody was going on about drowning in someone's eyes. It struck me as daft at the time but now, when I try to figure out why I permitted what happened that night to happen, I remember Gilbert's eyes and I think I know what that writer meant.

Anyway, I found myself standing by the bed and I couldn't tear my eyes away from his. He didn't say anything but he made a motion with his head and I knew he wanted me to kneel down. I felt sick and weak and unreal. As I went down on one knee I was back in infant school, doing the crib scene in the Nativity Play. I was the first shepherd, kneeling at the manger with the star above and Mary and Joseph behind, watching. It only lasted a second, and then Gilbert leant forward and his lips parted and I saw why he couldn't talk. His mouth was crammed with spikes.

I won't go on about it. As soon as I saw that mouth I knew what he was, but by then it was too late. He took what he wanted from me and now I'm one of them, like Stephanie Williams and the other chosen. We all make the trip out to the Melton place once a month – each on a separate night of course. We have to go, or we'd die like everybody else.

I expect you're wondering what it's like. Well, you don't feel that much different really, except you've no energy and the light hurts and you see colours as sort of faded. There're a lot more of us about than you think, by the way – so many that you're bound to know at least one. He'll be pasty-faced and a bit flabby, and not too particular about his clothes. He'll be irritable a lot of the time and he won't smile much. You'll probably wonder what he does for fun, or if he even knows what fun is. You might wonder why he bothers to go on living at all, and he'll certainly wonder himself sometimes. I do.

And I suppose the answer is that life's precious, and we tend to cling on to it even if we're not enjoying it. Whether I'll feel that way a thousand years from now remains to be seen. A thousand years is a lot of mince pies.

The Lost Boy

George Mackay Brown

There was one light in the village on Christmas Eve; it came from Jock Scabra's cottage, and he was the awk- wardest old man that had ever lived in our village or in the island, or in the whole of Orkney.

I was feeling very wretched and very ill-natured myself that evening. My Aunty Belle had just been explaining to me after tea that Santa Claus, if he did exist, was a spirit that moved people's hearts to generosity and goodwill; no more or less.

Gone was my fat apple-cheeked red-coated friend of the past ten winters. Scattered were the reindeer, broken the sledge that had beaten such a marvellous path through the constellations and the Merry Dancers, while all the children of Orkney slept. Those merry perilous descents down the lum, Yule eve by Yule eve, with the sack of toys and books, games and chocolate boxes, had never really taken place at all . . . I looked over towards our hearth, after my aunt had finished speaking: the magic had left it, it was only a place of peat flames and peat smoke.

I can't tell you how angry I was, the more I thought about it. How deceitful, how cruel, grown-ups were! They had exiled my dear old friend, Santa Claus, to eternal oblivion. The gifts I would find in my stocking next morning would have issued from Aunty Belle's 'spirit of generosity'. It was not the same thing at all. (Most of the year I saw little enough of that spirit of generosity – at Halloween, for example, she had boxed my ears till I saw stars that had never been in the sky, for stealing a few apples and nuts out of the cupboard, before 'dooking' time.)

If there was a more ill-tempered person than my Aunty-Belle in the village, it was, as I said, old Jock Scabra, the fisherman with a silver ring in his ear and a fierce one-eyed tom cat.

His house, alone in the village, was lit that night. I saw it, from our front door, at eleven o'clock.

Aunty Belle's piece of common sense had so angered me, that I was in a state of rebellion and recklessness. No, I would *not* sleep. I would not even stay in a house from which Santa had been banished. I felt utterly betrayed and bereaved.

When, about half past ten, I heard rending snores coming from Aunty Belle's bedroom, I got out of bed stealthily and put my cold clothes on, and unlatched the front door and went outside. The whole house had betrayed me – well, I intended to be out of the treacherous house when the magic hour of midnight struck.

The road through the village was deep in snow, dark except where under old Scabra's window the lamplight had stained it an orange colour. The snow shadows were blue under his walls. The stars were like sharp nails. Even though I had wrapped my scarf twice round my neck, I shivered in the bitter night.

Where could I go? The light in the old villian's

window was entrancing – I fluttered towards it like a moth. How would such a sour old creature be celebrating Christmas Eve? Thinking black thoughts, beside his embers, stroking his wicked one-eyed cat.

The snow crashed like thin fragile glass under my feet.

I stood at last outside the fisherman's window. I looked in.

What I saw was astonishing beyond ghosts or trows.

There was no crotchety old man inside, no one-eyed cat, no ingrained filth and hung cobwebs. The paraffin lamp threw a circle of soft light, and all that was gathered inside that radiance was clean and pristine: the cups and plates on the dresser, the clock and ship-in-the-bottle and tea-caddies on the mantelpiece, the framed picture of Queen Victoria on the wall, the blue stones of the floor, the wood and straw of the fireside chair, the patchwork quilt on the bed.

A boy I had never seen before was sitting at the table. He might have been about my own age, and his head was a mass of bronze ringlets. On the table in front of him were an apple, an orange, a little sailing ship crudely cut from wood with linen sails probably cut from an old shirt. The boy – whoever he was – considered those objects with the utmost gravity. Once he put out his finger and touched the hull of the toy ship; as if it was so precious it had to be treated with special delicacy, lest it broke like a soap-bubble. I couldn't see the boy's face – only his bright hair, his lissom neck, and the gravity and joy that informed all his gestures. These were his meagre Christmas presents, silently he rejoiced in them.

Beyond the circle of lamp-light, were there other

dwellers in the house? There may have been hidden breath in the darkened box bed in the corner.

I don't know how long I stood in the bitter night outside. My hands were trembling. I looked down at them – they were blue with cold.

Then suddenly, for a second, the boy inside the house turned his face to the window. Perhaps he had heard the tiny splinterings of snow under my boots, or my quickened heartbeats.

The face that looked at me was Jock Scabra's, but Jock Scabra's from far back at the pure source of his life, sixty winters ago, before the ring was in his ear and before bad temper and perversity had grained black lines and furrows into his face. It was as if a cloth had been taken to a tarnished web-clogged mirror.

The boy turned back, smiling, to his Christmas hoard.

I turned and went home. I lifted the latch quietly, not to awaken Aunty Belle – for, if she knew what I had been up to that midnight, there would have been little of her 'spirit of generosity' for me. I crept, trembling, into bed.

When I woke up on Christmas morning, the 'spirit of the season' had loaded my stocking and the chair beside the bed with boxes of sweets, a Guinness Book of Records, a digital watch, a game of space wars, a cowboy hat, and a 50 pence piece. Aunty Belle stood at my bedroom door, smiling. And, 'A Merry Christmas,' she said.

Breakfast over, I couldn't wait to get back to the Scabra house. The village was taken over by children with apples, snowballs, laughter as bright as bells.

I peered in at the window. All was as it had been. The piratical old man sluiced the last of his breakfast tea down his throat from a cracked saucer. He fell to picking his black-and-yellow teeth with a kipper-bone. His house was like a midden.

The one-eyed cat yawned wickedly beside the new flames in the hearth.

Not at Home
Jean Richardson

There were no lights in the bike shed and the bushes round about, which in daylight were an insignificant school-uniform green, loomed menacingly and cast fingers of shadow over the path.

Fetching her bike was the thing Alison hated most about staying late at school, though she usually had Joanne's cheerful company and the two of them together were brave enough to enjoy a few shivers. But Joanne had a sore throat, and although she had insisted on coming to school because it was English and she wanted her essay back, she had no voice for choir practice.

'But it was worth it,' she told Alison, her face flushed with pleasure and a temperature. '"A-minus and a nice feeling for words."'

It would have been showing off in anyone else, but Alison knew how much being good at English mattered to Joanne. It made up for not being good at sport and a coward at vaulting and climbing a rope.

'You'd be up it fast enough if there was a fire,' Miss Barry had said unsympathetically, and several girls who were jealous of Joanne had tittered.

But Joanne didn't care. She felt she was the wrong shape to climb a rope and saw herself, in an emergency, being saved by a handsome fireman. She was always making up stories. It was she who referred to the old bike at the far end of the shed as a skeleton and suggested that the school caretaker lurked there after dark, hoping to catch a nice plump little girl for his supper.

It was nonsense, of course. Old Trayner didn't look very attractive, with decayed teeth that you couldn't help noticing when he smiled, but he was probably lonely and only wanted someone to talk to.

Nevertheless Alison was in a greater hurry than usual to find the key to her padlock. She had been late that morning and the only space had been at the far end, next to the 'skeleton'. No one knew whose bike it was nor why it had been abandoned, but the mud-guards and chain had gone and the rust and cobwebs had moved in. Cobwebs . . . Spiders . . .

Alison jerked her bike free. In her hurry she had forgotten to remove her front lamp, and someone had nicked it. Blast! It was fatal to leave a lamp or a pump behind. Trayner probably had a thriving business in lamps and pumps, though most people suspected Finn's gang, who all had sticky fingers. Oh well, perhaps Dad would get her a dynamo at last.

She fumbled in her satchel for her safety belt. Books, ruler, Biros, and something that felt like crumbs or sand. No, it wasn't there. Then she remembered that it had wrapped itself round a book and she had put it in her desk. The door was probably still unlocked, but she didn't fancy crossing the dark hall and going upstairs and along the corridor to 2B. Schools were designed to be full of people; empty they were scary places, unnaturally quiet, as though everyone was dead. She'd have to do without her belt. It surely wouldn't matter just for once, though she had promised to wear it every day. It was something her mother had insisted on when she agreed to let Alison cycle to school.

She wedged her satchel in her basket and patted her saddle. Although she wouldn't have admitted it to Joanne, Alison thought of her bike as a trusty steed, and it was comforting to feel that she had an ally who would help her make a quick getaway.

She decided to risk cycling down the drive. They were not supposed to, but there were no lights in the head's study and she doubted whether Miss Cliffe, who lived opposite the school and was fond of keeping an eye on things even when off duty, would be glued to her window on a winter evening. More likely she'd be toasting her sturdy legs in front of the fire.

It seemed much darker without a front lamp, though its light was only small and wavering. The damp air tangled Alison's hair into frizzy curls and she shivered. They didn't have real fogs nowadays, not the kind you read about in Dickens, where people had to grope their way through the streets, but there were rags of mist and the street lamps had garish yellow haloes.

Alison sang to herself as she cycled along.

'The holly bears a berry as red as any blood,

And Mary bore sweet Jesus Christ

for to do poor sinners good.'

They had been practising for the end-of-term concert, and her head rang with glorias and tidings of comfort and joy. It was less than a month to Christmas, and the very thought warmed her.

She reached a crossroads and now had to turn right

into the main road. It was always a moment she dreaded, because the traffic raced along and she hadn't the nerve to take a quick chance.

She looked to the right, to the left, and then to the right again and stuck her arm out, though it seemed daft to signal when she wasn't very visible. She was halfway across when a car shot out impatiently from the other side of the crossroads. Startled, Alison swerved and then wobbled as her shoe slipped off the pedal and grazed the road, and at that moment a container lorry as tall as a house and as long as a train came hurtling towards her. It was going fast, and the swish of its hot breath seemed to suck her in towards the giant tyres. It happened so quickly: she felt as though she were being drawn more into a black void while two red eyes, which she realized afterwards must have been the brake lights of the car, blazed fiercely before being extinguished by the mist.

And then Alison found herself alone in the road. She was trembling, and she felt off-balance and as though her body didn't quite belong to her. Her heart was still pounding as she began to push her bike along, but it was too far to walk all the way. 'It's like falling off a horse,' she told herself. 'I must get on again or I shall lose my nerve.'

If only Mum would be there when she got home, but her mother worked part-time and had a late meeting. Peter might be home, but he wasn't prepared to say what he was up to these days, at least not to a sister. Alison enjoyed getting her own tea, but having the house all to herself was a bit creepy, especially at first, when it was so still she thought someone was there and holding his breath.

A container lorry came hurtling towards her

She turned into the Avenue, and took the third turning on the right and then down Fernhead. The houses were semi-detached, with bay windows and stubby front gardens behind privet hedges. Mum had promised to leave the light on, but she must have forgotten for the house was in darkness.

Alison pushed open the gate with her bike. The hedge seemed taller than usual and showered her with rain-drops. It really was time Dad cut it, though he always said as an excuse that hedges didn't grow in winter. She scrabbled in her pocket for the key. Soggy tissues . . . purse . . . the button off her raincoat . . . here it was. She felt for the lock and opened the door. The light switch was halfway along the wall, which meant that she had to plunge into blackness.

In her haste she banged her knee on something hard with a sharp corner. It took her by surprise and her heart thumped as she felt for the switch and pressed it down.

She had banged her knee on a large carved wooden chest that she had never seen before. She sensed at once that the hall was different. The carpet was the same. And there was that mark on it where Peter had upset a tin of paint. The walls were the same colour, but the two watercolours her gran had done on holiday were missing and in their place was a poster advertising a railway museum.

Alison looked round in bewilderment. She was in two minds about shutting the front door, because it seemed more frightening inside than out. Was she seeing things? Was she in the right house? She looked down at the telephone standing on the mysterious wooden chest and checked. Yes, it was the right number. Of course it was. Her mother was fond of saying they needed a change, and swapping round the pictures was just the sort of thing she liked doing. And it was just like her to forget to tell them that she'd bought a chest, because her father would then point out that they didn't need a chest because they'd got enough old junk of their own already. Yes, that must be what had happened.

She shut the front door and went upstairs to her room.

Only it wasn't her room any more. It belonged to someone who could have been about her age, but this person had a scarlet chest of drawers and wardrobe with a desk unit slotted between them. They were so much what Alison herself would have liked, that for a moment she wondered whether her parents had got rid of the old wardrobe that had belonged to Gran and the rickety table she used as a desk, and bought these smart units as a giant Christmas present.

But what had they done with her things? The clothes spilling out of the wardrobe weren't hers. She didn't wear long skirts or that vivid shade of pink. And what had Mum done with her books and the old toys that she couldn't bear to throw away . . . ?

She went along the landing into Peter's room. It was even untidier than usual: there were stacks of computer magazines and a workbench strewn with little tins of paint and brushes and glue and a half-finished model aeroplane. That was something Peter would never have the patience to make.

Alison was standing in the doorway of her parents' transformed bedroom when she heard the front door open.

It must be Peter, and she was about to call out and run downstairs to him when something stopped her. Everything was so different, so unexpected, that perhaps Peter might be changed in some dreadful way too.

She tiptoed across to the stairs, aware that she didn't want to be seen. She heard voices, and then someone slammed the front door.

'Danny! You've let the cat out.' It was a woman's voice.

'It wasn't my fault. He ran out before I could stop him.' The boy sounded younger than Peter.

'Well, don't blame me if he gets run over. You know how dangerous that road is. The Walkers' cat was killed last week and the traffic shoots along now it's one-way.'

'It doesn't make any difference if you let him out at the back. He's learned how to get round.' This was a girl, who went into the front room and switched on the television while the boy and the woman disappeared into the kitchen. Alison heard a tap running and then the sound of a kettle being plugged in.

She felt an intruder. They sounded like a normal family coming back to their own home, and what would they do when they found a stranger there? Would they believe that it had been her home that morning, that she and her brother and her parents had lived there for the past seven years? More likely they'd think she'd broken in and send for the police. And would *they* believe her? Alison saw herself trying to convince a disbelieving unsympathetic inspector that she had left the house that very morning and that the key that opened the front door was hers . . .

No, she must get out of the house as quickly as possible.

'It's upstairs. I'll go and get it.' The boy appeared in the hall and Alison ducked back into her bedroom. She held her breath as she heard him run up the stairs. Please let whatever he wanted be in his own room!

The door was just open, and she saw the boy go past with a jersey. There was a smell of frying, and Alison thought longingly of her own tea. She had been planning to have fish fingers and baked beans with oven-ready chips.

'In here or in there?' called the woman.

'In here. I want to watch telly.'

'Well, come and get it.'

There was a clatter of knives and forks and people went to and from the kitchen. Alison moved to the top of the stairs. The front room door was shut and they all seemed to be in there having their tea. Please don't let them have forgotten the salt or the ketchup!

She slid down the stairs, ran to the front door and out into the night. Something jumped on her and she half-screamed before she realized that it was the cat. It was as startled as she was, and fled under the hedge.

At least her bike was still there, invisible in the shadows. She grabbed it and stumbled out into the street. There seemed to be more traffic than usual, coming towards her on both sides of the road, and she remembered the woman saying that it was a one-way street. But it hadn't been. Not that morning.

I must have made a mistake, she told herself. It's the wrong street but somehow my key fitted their front door. Was it possible? But the phone number was the right one and the sign at the end of the street, when she reached it, said unmistakably 'Fernhead Road'.

Alison was near to tears. She was cold and frightened and alone, and she longed for her mother and the safety and security of her own home. Even Peter would have been welcome. He must be due home whatever he'd been up to, and he would find everything changed as she had done.

She cycled past the little public garden that always shut early in winter. That at least looked the same. She was now approaching the high street where there was a straggling parade of shops. There was Aziz where they bought sweets and newspapers, the Chinese takeaway, a fish and chip shop and a pub called The Frog and Nightdress. There couldn't be another pub with a name like that! Home must be somewhere nearby. Perhaps if she were to go back to Fernhead Road she would find that it had all been some ghastly mistake or a bad dream.

And then Alison saw that something had changed. On Saturday she had noticed a new hoarding that had gone up on some waste ground at one end of the shops. It said that the site had been acquired by a chain of supermarkets and now, only four days later, there was the new supermarket.

Wonderingly she wheeled her bike towards it. There was even a rack of cycles outside, and as though in a dream she parked hers and went in.

It was the largest supermarket she had ever seen. Avenues of shelves stretched away into the distance and frozen cabinets half a mile long were stacked with regiments of turkeys, ducks and geese. Boxes of mince pies and Christmas puddings were stacked in a pyramid crowned by a plastic Christmas tree with winking lights, and a carol, arranged for some vast invisible orchestra, wafted through the air as though on the wings of an aerosol.

Most of the customers wheeled trolleys piled so high that they might have been shopping for expeditions to the North Pole or the Andes, while boys in holly-green aprons replenished the shelves or hurried up and down the aisles checking queries relayed to them by two-way radio. Some of them didn't look much older than Alison, and she tried to pluck up the courage to speak to a boy who was shovelling brazils into a counter of nuts. There was something familiar about him, she realized. He reminded her of Sean Maloney, who was in her class, but it couldn't be him because they weren't allowed to take jobs, even part-time. She knew there were lots of Maloneys, so he must be an older brother with the same tight coppery curls.

But what could she say? He'd think she was a nutter if she asked him how they could possibly have built, stocked and staffed a supermarket in four days!

She had just decided to ask him, as an opener, where the milk was, when she saw a familiar face further down the aisle. It was Joanne's mother, Mrs Cullen, and she was reaching for some mince pies.

It was better than the best Christmas present. Everything was going to be all right, even if it was rather puzzling. She would tell Mrs Cullen about the house and perhaps go back and have tea with Joanne while it was all sorted out.

She ran down the aisle. Mrs Cullen had her back to Alison so didn't see her coming.

'Mrs Cullen, am I glad to see you. I don't know what's happened –'

Alison got no further, because when Joanne's mother saw her, she made a funny little choking noise and crumpled up as though Alison had shot her. She fell against the display and mince pies and Christmas puddings skated along the aisles while the tree lurched forward, its lights flashing a wild signal of distress.

'She's having a fit,' said one woman. 'I think she's fainted,' said another, but neither of them made any move to help. A girl from the checkout, who had done a course in first aid, propped up Mrs Cullen and asked for a glass of water.

Mrs Cullen opened her eyes. She seemed dazed.

'I think she's only fainted,' said the checkout girl. 'Can someone get a chair?'

Sean Maloney, looking a mixture of embarrassed and inquisitive, brought one.

Mrs Cullen recognized him. 'Did you see her?' she asked faintly.

'See who?'

'That girl. The one who came up to me. She . . . she . . .' Mrs Cullen was crying.

'I didn't see any girl.' Several customers were looking at Sean as though he were somehow to blame.

'It wasn't *any* girl. You must remember her. She was in your class. She was Joanne's friend. Alison Potter.'

'Alison Potter!' Sean Maloney backed away. 'But it couldn't have been her. She was . . .' He didn't like to say it.

'Killed,' said Mrs Cullen with a shudder. 'That's right. She was run over and killed on the way home from school. The Potters lived in our road, but they moved after the accident.'

'You must have imagined it,' said Sean. 'Or seen someone who looked like her.'

He looked round at the shoppers, most of whom had moved away now that there was nothing to see but a frightened-looking woman on a chair. He remembered Alison Potter, but there was no sign of her, or of any girl who looked remotely like her.

Rummins
Roald Dahl

The sun was up over the hills now and the mist had cleared and it was wonderful to be striding along the road with the dog in the early morning, especially when it was autumn, with the leaves changing to gold and yellow and sometimes one of them breaking away and falling slowly, turning slowly over in the air, dropping noiselessly right in front of him on to the grass beside the road. There was a small wind up above, and he could hear the beeches rustling and murmuring like a crowd of people.

This was always the best time of the day for Claud Cubbage. He gazed approvingly at the rippling velvety hindquarters of the greyhound trotting in front of him.

'Jackie,' he called softly. 'Hey, Jackson. How you feeling, boy?'

The dog half turned at the sound of its name and gave a quick acknowledging wag of the tail.

There would never be another dog like this Jackie, he told himself. How beautiful the slim streamlining, the small pointed head, the yellow eyes, the black mobile nose. Beautiful the long neck, the way the deep brisket curved back and up out of sight into no stomach at all. See how he walked upon his toes, noiselessly, hardly touching the surface of the road at all.

'Jackson,' he said. 'Good old Jackson.'

In the distance, Claud could see Rummins' farm-house, small, narrow, and ancient, standing back behind the hedge on the right-hand side.

I'll turn round there, he decided. That'll be enough for today.

Rummins, carrying a pail of milk across the yard, saw him coming down the road. He set the pail down slowly and came forward to the gate, leaning both arms on the topmost bar, waiting.

'Morning, Mr Rummins,' Claud said. It was necessary to be polite to Rummins because of eggs.

Rummins nodded and leaned over the gate, looking critically at the dog.

'Looks well,' he said.

'He is well.'

'When's he running?'

'I don't know, Mr Rummins.'

'Come on. When's he running?'

'He's only ten months yet, Mr Rummins. He's not even schooled properly, honest.'

The small beady eyes of Rummins peered sus-piciously over the top of the gate. Claud moved his feet uncomfortably on the black road surface. He disliked very much this man with the wide frog mouth, the broken teeth, the shifty eyes; and most of all he disliked having to be polite to him because of eggs.

'That hayrick of yours opposite,' he said, searching desperately for another subject. 'It's full of rats.'

'All hayricks got rats.'

'Not like this one. Matter of fact we've been having a touch of trouble with the authorities about that.'

Rummins glanced up sharply. He didn't like trouble

with the authorities. Any man who sells eggs black-market and kills pigs without a permit is wise to avoid contact with that sort of people.

'What kind of trouble?'

'They sent the ratcatcher along.'

'You mean just for a few rats?'

'A few! Blimey, it's *swarming*!'

'Never.'

'Honest it is, Mr Rummins. There's hundreds of 'em.'

'Didn't the ratcatcher catch 'em?'

'No.'

'Why?'

'I reckon they're too artful.'

Rummins began thoughtfully to explore the inner rim of one nostril with the end of his thumb, holding the noseflap between thumb and finger as he did so.

'I wouldn't give thank you for no ratcatchers,' he said. 'Ratcatchers is government men working for the soddin' government and I wouldn't give thank you for 'em.'

'Nor me, Mr Rummins. All ratcatchers is slimy cunning creatures.'

'Well,' Rummins said, sliding fingers under his cap to scratch the head, 'I was coming over soon anyway to fetch in that rick. Reckon I might just as well do it today as any other time. I don't want no government men nosing around my stuff thank you very much.'

'Exactly, Mr Rummins.'

'We'll be over later – Bert and me.' With that he turned and ambled off across the yard.

Around three in the afternoon, Rummins and Bert were seen riding slowly up the road in a cart drawn by a ponderous and magnificent black carthorse. Opposite the filling-station the cart turned off into the field and stopped near the hayrick.

'This ought to be worth seeing,' I said. 'Get the gun.'

Claud fetched the rifle and slipped a cartridge into the breech.

I strolled across the road and leaned against the open gate. Rummins was on the top of the rick now and cutting away at the cord that bound the thatching. Bert remained in the cart, fingering the four-foot-long knife.

Bert had something wrong with one eye. It was pale grey all over, like a boiled fish-eye, and although it was motionless in its socket it appeared always to be looking at you and following you round the way the eyes of the people in some of those portraits do, in the museums. Wherever you stood and wherever Bert was looking, there was this faulty eye fixing you sideways with a cold stare, boiled and misty pale with a black dot in the centre, like a fish-eye on a plate.

In his build he was the opposite of his father who was short and squat like a frog. Bert was a tall, reedy, boneless boy, loose at the joints, even the head loose upon the shoulders, falling sideways as though perhaps it was too heavy for the neck.

'You only made this rick last June,' I said to him. 'Why take it away so soon?'

'Dad wants it.'

'Funny time to cut a new rick, November.'

'Dad wants it,' Bert repeated, and both his eyes, the sound one and the other stared down at me with a look of absolute vacuity.

'Going to all that trouble stacking it and thatching it and then pulling it down five months later.'

'Dad wants it.' Bert's nose was running and he kept wiping it with the back of his hand and wiping the back of the hand on his trousers.

'Come on, Bert,' Rummins called, and the boy climbed up on to the rick and stood in the place where the thatch had been removed. He took the knife and began to cut down into the tight-packed hay with an easy-swinging, sawing movement, holding the handle with both hands and rocking his body like a man sawing wood with a big saw. I could hear the crisp cutting noise of the blade against the dry hay and the noise becoming softer as the knife sank deeper into the rick.

'Claud's going to take a pot at the rats as they come out.'

The man and the boy stopped abruptly and looked across the road at Claud who was leaning against the red pump with rifle in hand.

'Tell him to put that rifle away,' Rummins said.

'He's a good shot. He won't hit you.'

'No one's potting no rats alongside of me, don't matter how good they are.'

'You'll insult him.'

'Tell him to put it away,' Rummins said, slow and hostile. 'I don't mind dogs nor sticks but I'll not have rifles.'

The two on the hayrick watched while Claud did as he was told, then they resumed their work in silence. Soon Bert came down into the cart, and reaching out with both hands he pulled a slice of solid hay away from the rick so that it dropped neatly into the cart beside him.

A rat, grey-black, with a long tail, came out of the base of the rick and ran into the hedge.

A rat came out of the base of the rick and ran into the hedge

'A rat,' I said.

'Kill it,' Rummins said. 'Why don't you get a stick and kill it?'

The alarm had been given now and the rats were coming out quicker, one or two of them every minute, fat and long-bodied, crouching close to the ground as they ran through the grass into the hedge. Whenever the horse saw one of them it twitched its ears and followed it with uneasy rolling eyes.

Bert had climbed back on top of the rick and was cutting out another bale. Watching him, I saw him suddenly stop, hesitate for perhaps a second, then again begin to cut, but very cautiously this time, and now I could hear a different sound, a muffled rasping noise as the blade of the knife grated against something hard.

Bert pulled out the knife and examined the blade, testing it with his thumb. He put it back, letting it down gingerly into the cut, feeling gently downward until it came again upon the hard object; and once more, when he made another cautious little sawing movement, there came that grating sound.

Rummins turned his head and looked over his shoulder at the boy. He was in the act of lifting an armful of loosened thatch, bending forward with both hands grasping the straw, but he stopped dead in the middle of what he was doing and looked at Bert. Bert remained still, hands holding the handle of the knife, a look of bewilderment on his face. Behind, the sky was a pale clear blue and the two figures up there on the hayrick stood out sharp and black like an etching against the paleness.

Then Rummins' voice, louder than usual, edged with an unmistakable apprehension that the loudness did nothing to conceal: 'Some of them haymakers is too bloody careless what they put on a rick these days.'

He paused, and again the silence, the men motionless, and across the road Claud leaning motionless against the red pump. It was so quiet suddenly we could hear a woman's voice far down the valley on the next farm calling the men to food.

Then Rummins again, shouting where there was no need to shout: 'Go on, then! Go on an' cut through it, Bert! A little stick of wood won't hurt the soddin' knife!'

For some reason, as though perhaps scenting trouble, Claud came strolling across the road and joined me leaning on the gate. He didn't say anything, but both of us seemed to know that there was something disturbing about these two men, about the stillness that surrounded them and especially about Rummins himself. Rummins was frightened. Bert was frightened too. And now as I watched them, I became conscious of a small vague image moving just below the surface of my memory. I tried desperately to reach back and grasp it. Once I almost touched it, but it slipped away and when I went after it I found myself travelling back and back through many weeks, back into the yellow days of summer – the warm wind blowing down the valley from the south, the big beech trees heavy with their foliage, the fields turning to gold, the harvesting, the haymaking, the rick – the building of the rick.

Instantly I felt a fine electricity of fear running over the skin of my stomach.

Yes – the building of the rick. When was it we had built it? June? That was it, of course – a hot muggy day in June with the clouds low overhead and the air thick with the smell of thunder.

And Rummins had said, 'Let's for God's sake get it in quick before the rain comes.'

And Ole Jimmy had said, 'There ain't going to be no rain. And there ain't no hurry either. You know very well when thunder's in the south it don't cross over into the valley.'

Rummins, standing up in the cart handing out the pitchforks, had not answered him. He was in a furious brooding temper because of his anxiety about getting in the hay before it rained.

'There ain't gin' to be no rain before evening,' Ole Jimmy had repeated, looking at Rummins; and Rummins had stared back at him, the eyes glimmering with a slow anger.

All through the morning we had worked without a pause, loading the hay into the cart, trundling it across the field, pitching it out on to the slowly growing rick that stood over by the gate opposite the filling-station. We could hear the thunder in the south as it came towards us and moved away again. Then it seemed to return and remain stationary somewhere beyond the hills, rumbling intermittently. When we looked up we could see the clouds overhead moving and changing shape in the turbulence of the upper air; but on the ground it was hot and muggy and there was no breath of wind. We worked slowly, listlessly in the heat, shirts wet with sweat, faces shining.

Claud and I had worked beside Rummins on the rick itself, helping to shape it, and I could remember how very hot it had been and the flies around my face and the sweat pouring out everywhere; and especially

I could remember the grim scowling presence of Rummins beside me, working with a desperate urgency and watching the sky and shouting at the men to hurry.

At noon, in spite of Rummins, we had knocked off for lunch.

Claud and I had sat down under the hedge with Ole Jimmy and another man called Wilson who was a soldier home on leave, and it was too hot to do much talking. Wilson had some bread and cheese and a canteen of cold tea. Ole Jimmy had a satchel that was an old gas-mask container, and in this, closely packed, standing upright with their necks protruding, were six pint bottles of beer.

'Come on,' he said, offering a bottle to each of us.

'I'd like to buy one from you,' Claud said, knowing very well the old man had little money.

'Take it.'

'I must pay you.'

'Don't be so daft. Drink it.'

He was a very good old man, good and clean, with a clean pink face that he shaved each day. He had used to be a carpenter, but they retired him at the age of seventy and that was some years before. Then the Village Council, seeing him still active, had given him the job of looking after the newly built children's playground, of maintaining the swings and see-saws in good repair and also of acting as a kind of gentle watchdog, seeing that none of the kids hurt themselves or did anything foolish.

That was a fine job for an old man to have and everybody seemed pleased with the way things were going – until a certain Saturday night. That night

Ole Jimmy had got drunk and gone reeling and singing down the middle of the High Street with such a howling noise that people got out of their beds to see what was going on below. The next morning they had sacked him, saying he was a waster and a drunkard not fit to associate with young children on the playground.

But then an astonishing thing happened. The first day that he stayed away – a Monday it was – not one single child came near the playground.

Nor the next day, nor the one after that.

All week the swings and the see-saws and the high slide with steps going up to it stood deserted. Not a child went near them. Instead they followed Ole Jimmy out into a field behind the Rectory and played their games there with him watching; and the result of all this was that after a while the Council had no alternative but to give the old man back his job.

He still had it now and he still got drunk and no one said anything about it any more. He left it only for a few days each year, at haymaking time. All his life Ole Jimmy had loved to go haymaking and he wasn't going to give it up yet.

'You want one?' he asked now, holding a bottle out to Wilson, the soldier.

'No thanks. I got tea.'

'They say tea's good on a hot day.'

'It is. Beer makes me sleepy.'

'If you like,' I said to Ole Jimmy, 'we could walk across to the filling-station and I'll do you a couple of nice sandwiches? Would you like that?'

'Beer's plenty. There's more food in one bottle of beer, me lad, than twenty sandwiches.'

He smiled at me, showing two rows of pale-pink, toothless gums, but it was a pleasant smile and there was nothing repulsive about the way the gums showed.

We sat for a while in silence. The soldier finished his bread and cheese and lay back on the ground, tilting his hat forward over his face. Ole Jimmy had drunk three bottles of beer, and now he offered the last to Claud and me.

'No thanks.'

'No thanks. One's plenty for me.'

The old man shrugged, unscrewed the stopper, tilted his head back and drank, pouring the beer into his mouth with the lips held open so the liquid ran smoothly without gurgling down his throat. He wore a hat that was of no colour at all and of no shape, and it did not fall off when he tilted back his head.

'Ain't Rummins goin' to give that old horse a drink?' he asked, lowering the bottle, looking across the field at the great carthorse that stood steaming between the shafts of the cart.

'Not Rummins.'

'Horses is thirsty, just the same as us.' Ole Jimmy paused, still looking at the horse. 'You got a bucket of water in that place of yours there?'

'Of course.'

'No reason why we shouldn't give the old horse a drink then, is there?'

'That's a very good idea. We'll give him a drink.'

Claud and I both stood up and began walking towards the gate, and I remember turning and calling to the old man: 'You quite sure you wouldn't like me to bring you a nice sandwich? Won't take a second to make.'

He shook his head and waved the bottle at us and said something about taking himself a little nap. We went on through the gate over the road to the filling station.

I suppose we stayed away for about an hour attending to customers and getting ourselves something to eat, and when at length we returned, Claud carrying the bucket of water, I noticed that the rick was at least six foot high.

'Some water for the old horse,' Claud said, looking hard at Rummins who was up in the cart pitching hay on to the rick.

The horse put its head in the bucket, sucking and blowing gratefully at the water.

'Where's Ole Jimmy?' I asked. We wanted the old man to see the water because it had been his idea.

When I asked the question there was a moment, a brief moment, when Rummins hesitated, pitchfork in mid-air, looking around him.

'I brought him a sandwich,' I added.

'Bloody old fool drunk too much beer and gone off home to sleep,' Rummins said.

I strolled along the hedge back to the place where we had been sitting with Ole Jimmy. The five empty bottles were lying there in the grass. So was the satchel. I picked up the satchel and carried it back to Rummins.

'I don't think Ole Jimmy's gone home, Mr Rummins,' I said, holding up the satchel by the long shoulder-band. Rummins glanced at it but made no reply. He was in a frenzy of haste now because the thunder was closer, the clouds blacker, the heat more oppressive than ever.

Carrying the satchel, I started back to the filling-station where I remained for the rest of the afternoon, serving customers. Towards evening, when the rain came, I glanced across the road and noticed that they had got the hay in and were laying a tarpaulin over the rick.

In a few days the thatcher arrived and took the tarpaulin off and made a roof of straw instead. He was a good thatcher and he made a fine roof with long straw, thick and well packed. The slope was nicely angled, the edges cleanly clipped, and it was a pleasure to look at it from the road or from the door of the filling-station.

All this came flooding back to me now as clearly as if it were yesterday – the building of the rick on that hot thundery day in June, the yellow field, the sweet woody smell of the hay; and Wilson the soldier, with tennis shoes on his feet, Bert with the boiled eye, Ole Jimmy with the clean old face, the pink naked gums; and Rummins, the broad dwarf, standing up in the cart scowling at the sky because he was anxious about the rain.

At this very moment, there he was again, this Rummins, crouching on top of the rick with a sheaf of thatch in his arms looking round at the son, the tall Bert, motionless also, both of them black like silhouettes against the sky, and once again I felt the fine electricity of fear as it came and went in little waves over the skin of my stomach.

'Go on and cut through it, Bert,' Rummins said, speaking loudly.

Bert put pressure on the big knife and there was a high grating noise as the edge of the blade sawed across something hard. It was clear from Bert's face that he did not like what he was doing.

It took several minutes before the knife was through – then again at last the softer sound of the blade slicing the tight-packed hay and Bert's face turned sideways to the father, grinning with relief, nodding inanely.

'Go on and cut it out,' Rummins said, and still he did not move.

Bert made a second vertical cut the same depth as the first; then he got down and pulled the bale of hay so it came away cleanly from the rest of the rick like a chunk of cake, dropping into the cart at his feet.

Instantly the boy seemed to freeze, staring stupidly at the newly exposed face of the rick, unable to believe or perhaps refusing to believe what this thing was that he had cut in two.

Rummins, who knew very well what it was, had turned away and was climbing quickly down the other side of the rick. He moved so fast he was through the gate and halfway across the road before Bert started to scream.

Left in the Dark
John Gordon

The village seemed to be stitched into the hills. A cluster of houses was held by the thread of the stream, and the stream itself was caught under a bridge and hooked around a stone barn in a fold of the heather and bracken. In the October sunshine the hills looked as soft as a quilt.

'There it is,' said the big lady sitting at the front of the bus near the driver. 'Lastingford.'

'Me Mam'll never remember that,' said Alec to Jack alongside him. 'She'll never have room to get it on the envelope.'

'It's worse than that, man,' said Jack. 'I don't suppose they even get the post out here.'

The lady had heard them and she stood up and turned round so that she could talk to the whole bus. 'Now I don't want any of you to get worried,' she said. 'The people here are just the same as anywhere else and I know they're going to make you welcome.' She smiled down at Alec and Jack. 'And you'll all be hearing from home because the post comes quite regularly.'

David, sitting by himself behind the other two, wanted her to look at him. She had been standing by the bus in Newcastle, ticking their names off on her list and watching as his Mam kissed him and his Dad shook his hand. Her rather large face under the green hat with the brim had the funny little smile that women gave before they burst into tears, and she had nodded to his mother, who was quite unable to speak, as he climbed aboard. But now she had gone bossy, nursing her clipboard like a baby, so he looked out of the window again, and carefully, so that nobody else could see, took the tears away from the corners of his eyes with his fingertips.

'Missus.' Jack got the lady's attention. 'Do they ever have bombs here?'

'No, of course they don't. That's why you're being evacuated. You'll be as safe as houses.'

David had seen a house come down. Half an hour after a bomb had landed, while the men in white helmets were climbing over fallen walls and jagged wood, the house next door had collapsed with its grey slates sliding like molten slag, and the smoke from the kitchen fire still coming from the chimney pot as it plunged in a gentle roar into the soft cloud of dust. Mrs Armstrong was dead under that, but he never saw her.

'So you've got nothing to worry about,' said the lady. 'There'll be cows and milk and horses.'

'And duck ponds?' Alec, with the very pale face and bright red hair, looked up at her innocently. 'With little ducks?'

She was not sure whether he was making fun of her, and blushed as she said, 'I wouldn't be surprised. You're in the countryside now, you know.'

'I love fluffy little ducks,' said Alec, and the lady pretended not to see as he and Jack put their heads together and choked to stop themselves laughing. She walked past them to the back of the bus.

That smaller boy, she thought, the one behind them, he wouldn't mind talking about ducks. But I can't say anything to him or they'll think he's a baby. Well he's not much more. She looked at her clipboard. He's only eight. She shook her head. It was bad enough for the other two, and they were three or four years older, but the little one should never be away from home.

They were going down into the valley now, but David could still see the hills humped like the green eiderdown on his bed at home where, first thing in the morning, he made landscapes of it and had adventures up and down its slopes.

The bus stopped in the mouth of a stony track between the pub and a shop that looked more like a house with all the goods stacked inside somebody's front room. There were two Boy Scouts on the bus, big lads who had come to help with the evacuees, and they were each given their own little group to shepherd, but the lady picked out Alec and Jack and David to come along with her. 'These three are together,' she told the Scouts. 'I'll just see them settled first.' And then she raised her voice so that everybody could hear. 'I'll be along to see every one of you and make sure you're all nice and comfy.' But some of the girls were crying. 'It's just like a holiday,' she said. 'The people here are really looking forward to having you. You'll see.' She looked up and down the steep road. One woman stood on her doorstep a little way down the street; otherwise there was nobody.

'Missus.' Jack caught the lady's attention. 'I've never been on holiday.'

A desperate gleam crossed her face. 'Never mind,' she said. Her voice had a tremble in it and her accent slipped so that she spoke like their mothers. 'Don't worry, pet, I'm going to take you to a really nice house. Now pick up your things.'

Jack had his clothes in a parcel, but Alec and David each had small suitcases, Alec's with a strap around it, and all three wore overcoats despite the heat of the October sun. They had come to stay, and winter was not far away.

The lady led them uphill and around a sharp corner into a rough road which climbed away steeply to the high hillside where sheep were placed like puffs of anti-aircraft smoke among the purple heather, but they turned sharply again, and a few paces took them to the front of a tall, plain-faced house of grey stone. Plants with broad leaves stood in the windows on each side of the door, and lace curtains hung like rain falling in the dark rooms behind. But the brass door knocker was brightly polished and the step was scrubbed almost white. The lady's hand was still reaching for the knocker when the door opened, pulled suddenly back, and a girl of about sixteen stood there, trying to see beyond the upstretched arm and at the same time saying, 'Hallo, have you brought them – the evacuees? There should be three, all little lads, Mrs Prosser said. Oh yes.'

As the words came tumbling out, her eyes had been alighting on each of them in turn, and counting. 'Good. They're all there.' Her round face beamed.

Her rosy cheeks and quick smile seemed to David to shine against the grey stone and dark hall behind her, and to be quite wrong for the clothes she wore. She had a white lace cap on her brown hair, which was drawn back into a bun, and she wore a black dress buttoned high at the neck, black stockings, and black low-heeled shoes so that her body seemed in a prison from which only her face, looking over the wall, was free. She bobbed a brief curtsy to the lady. 'Mrs Prosser says I'm to take them up to their room while she sees you in the parlour.'

The lady in the green hat stood to one side and let them go ahead of her, touching each on the shoulder as they went by as though what she really wanted to do was hold them back because they were barging into a place where they did not belong. 'Wipe your feet,' she said three times, once to each of them, and then came in behind them and stood quite still, clutching her clipboard, as the maid closed the door and shut out most of the light. The hall was dim and chilly.

Jack sniffed. 'Smells of polish,' he said. 'Look at the shine on that floor.'

A thin rug lay along the centre of the hall and Alec pushed at it with his toe so that it wrinkled over the polished wood. 'Could be dangerous if you came downstairs in a rush,' he said.

Jack also pushed at the carpet. 'Man!' he said loudly, 'you could go arse over tip on that!'

'Sh!' The lady was horrified, but the girl gave a little strangled squeak and went past them with her lips and eyes squeezed tight. She opened a door and they heard her mumble something and then hastily beckon the lady forward, show her through, and shut the door quickly behind her.

'You lot!' She held herself very upright, struggling not to laugh. 'If that's the way you're going to carry on you'll get me shot. Where's your manners?'

'But it's true,' said Jack. 'That floor's a danger.'

'And it's not the only thing that's dangerous around here.' She advanced on them, and her laughter was now well under control. 'If you don't watch your step, Mrs Prosser will get you sent away home again.'

'I won't mind,' said Jack.

'Nor me neither.' Alec backed him up.

'But what's to become of me?' She had her hands on her hips. 'If you gang don't watch your p's and q's, I'll get the blame and she'll get rid of me, and then what would I do without a job?' She looked at each of them as sternly as her round face would allow. 'Eh?'

David saw that the other two were going to stand dumbly, and he was suddenly afraid they would turn the one friendly face against them. 'We won't get you into trouble, Miss,' he said.

He stood partly behind the others and was the smallest. Her eyes rested on him fully for the first time and her expression suddenly melted. 'You don't call me Miss,' she said. 'I'm not old enough for that.'

Jack turned and looked down at David. 'Everybody knows that,' he said. 'Don't be daft.'

'No he's not.' The girl seemed suddenly to charge at them. 'He's not daft. He's the nicest little lad of the three of you. What's your name, pet?'

'David,' he said.

'Right then, David. We'll lead the way and let them follow.' She held out her hand and he longed to hold it but he knew that if he did the others would call him soft, so he stood firm and looked up at her sternly. Once again she had to hold back a giggle. 'Very well then, David,' she said, and turned to the other two to get their names. 'You can call me Pauline, but you better not be cheeky, or else I'll tell the Missus.'

She turned, and her face and cap were hidden so that her figure was entirely black and merged with the deep shadows at the end of the hall so completely that David thought she had vanished through some side doorway. Only the rustle of her dress drew him forward. Then she was climbing stairs much broader than in any house in his own street, and he hurried forward in case she should disappear again. She climbed swiftly and his heavy case bumped against his legs as he struggled to keep up with her. But when they came to a landing she waited for them. 'Are you out of puff?' she said. 'Because we've got a long way to go yet.'

There was a window with coloured glass. 'It's just like being in a church,' Jack said to her.

'And nearly as cold.' Alec shivered. 'Do you have hymns?'

'No music.' Pauline shook her head. 'The Missus doesn't like to hear anybody singing. She doesn't like any noise at all inside these four walls.'

The unseen Mrs Prosser could hardly have complained as they mounted the next flight and the next because the chatter from Alec and Jack died out as they became breathless, and the only sound was their feet on the stair carpet. But David noticed that as they climbed higher, and the noise was less likely to be heard down below, the carpet became thinner and their footsteps louder. And the stairway became narrower until there was scarcely enough room for them and their luggage, and their free hands were holding a painted rail. They came to a landing of bare boards and one small window.

'Can't be any farther, can it?' said Jack. 'We must be practically under the roof with the birdies.'

'That's where you're wrong, hinny.' Pauline imitated his Newcastle accent. 'There's one more stage yet.' She went to a plain door that had a latch instead of a handle. 'Lift the sneck,' she said as she raised the latch and pulled back the door, 'and here we are. Almost.'

She went into darkness and they heard her feet on the wooden treads of uncarpeted stairs, and then another door opened and let down a grey light on the first flight. 'Come on,' she called, and Jack pushed to the front. Alec did not want to be left on the bare landing and went next, leaving David where he was.

The door swung to and he was suddenly alone. The landing was like a little room, an empty cupboard, and no sound came from below or above, not even the scratch of a beetle. He had had a dream like this, an empty room in a house far away from anything he knew. He stood where he was and waited to wake up.

It was a full minute before Pauline, realizing he was left behind, came clattering down the stairs.

'Oh, poor little lad!' She was immediately alongside him, bending over with her arm around his shoulders. 'You'll break my heart, you will.' Her tears came to the surface but did not quite brim over. 'Standing there with your overcoat buttoned up and your case by your side. You look as though you're all alone on a railway station – little boy lost.' She was suddenly so motherly she even smoothed his dark hair. 'Why didn't you come after us?'

Until then he had not thought of crying, but now his mouth turned down at the corners. 'There was a man,' he said.

'A man? Where?'

He raised a hand and pointed towards the door. If she hadn't asked him, he was sure he would never have remembered what had just happened. But it was true. A big man had followed Alec through the door, and that was why he had hung back and been left alone.

'There's no man here,' said Pauline. 'Just us.'

'I saw him.' The man was tall and wore a brownish suit.

Pauline studied his face for a moment and then looked carefully around the landing. 'There's no man up here, David. There's no man in the whole house.'

David knew that. But he had seen the broad back and the speckled, rough material of the man's jacket and trousers. It was the sort of thing you see and don't see at the same time, and he would have forgotten it a moment later if it hadn't been for Pauline asking him. She was looking into his face now, as full of kindness as his mother, and his lip quivered.

'Oh,' she said, crouching to hug him, 'it's only your imagination, David, after all you've been through with that horrible Hitler bombing everybody. And we had to go and leave you all by yourself.' She pulled a handkerchief from her sleeve and wiped his eyes. 'But I can tell you this, pet, we'll never leave you alone up here again. Never, ever.'

Mrs Prosser had made sure that the three boys were going to be seen about the house as little as possible. Their room was in the attic, three iron beds in a row under a whitewashed, sloping ceiling.

'Just like a dormitory,' said Jack.

'It's quite nice.' Pauline was straightening bedclothes. 'I've tried to make it homely.' She had brought two rag rugs from home to put on the cold lino and, without Mrs Prosser knowing, had taken the curtains from another room at the top of the house and hung them in the single dormer window that jutted out from the slates of the roof.

'What's that?' Jack demanded, pointing to a table beneath the window.

'That's a wash-hand-stand. Don't you know anything?' A jug stood in a big basin on the table's marble top. 'That's where you put your soap.' She pointed to a china dish. 'And you hang your towels on these rails around the edge. I'll bring you up some water directly.'

'All of us in the same basin?' Alec didn't believe it. 'The water'll get black.'

'I bags first,' said Jack.

There was a chair with a cane bottom next to a huge wardrobe, but no other furniture. 'You can hang your clothes up in there later,' she told them, 'but now you've got to go and meet the Missus. Put your overcoats on your beds. No . . .' she stopped Jack throwing his coat on the middle bed '. . . that's for the smallest one. You two big lads have got to look after him.' Jack and Alec both pulled faces. 'And you needn't be like that, either.'

'Has he been crying for his Mam?' Jack looked carefully at David's face.

'No I haven't!' David lunged forward suddenly, and Jack had to fend him off as Pauline gave a shriek.

'He's a proper little fury when he's roused.' She was delighted with him. 'You'll have to watch your step.' Jack put his tongue out at her. 'And if there's any more of that you'll have me to deal with.'

'You're only a lass.'

'We'll see about that!' Suddenly she was chasing all three of them round the room and over the beds, until she caught Jack in a corner. 'Say sorry or I'll give you a Chinese burn.' She had her fist bunched ready to scrub her knuckles on his scalp. 'Say sorry!'

'I won't.'

They were struggling and laughing, when faintly, from far away, a bell tinkled. Through all the noise Pauline heard it and instantly pushed herself clear.

'Is my cap straight? Look at my dress – the state it's in! All crumpled up.' She was pushing her hair back and pressing at the creases at the same time. 'Come on now.' Her attitude had changed and she was ordering them to follow her. They even lined up before they went through the door. David was last again, and it was this that made him think of the man. He looked back. The room was quite empty. If there had been a man, the only place he could be was in the wardrobe. David clung to the back of Alec's jacket as he followed him down the stairs.

They came down through the house, their footsteps becoming quieter as the stair carpets thickened, and then they were in the hushed hall. Pauline smoothed her skirt once more, licked her lips, looked briefly at the three boys, and tapped at a door hidden in its own recess. They saw her bob a curtsy as she entered, then stand back and beckon them.

The light coming through the window was guillotined by the drape of the curtains, and when the door closed with a soft click behind him David felt trapped in a dark sea cave. Tall cabinets rose to the ceiling where they lipped over in black scrolls, and pictures in ebony frames leant from the walls like the mouths of great howling creatures held back by chains. His hand reached for Jack's and held it.

'Well?' The voice was a high-pitched yelp, and for a split second he thought he saw a dog in a dress. The grey face against the chair back had high cheekbones and a chin so thin it was like a dog's pointed muzzle. It barked again. 'Stop fidgeting, girl.'

The rustle of Pauline's dress ceased. David had half hidden himself behind Jack as they were lined up on one side of the wide fireplace, and the voice rattled again. 'I can hardly see one of them. Fetch him out.'

Pauline nudged him into the open.

'Are they clean?' The bony eyebrows turned away from them to the lady in the green hat who stood beside her chair.

'Of course they are, Mrs Prosser.' The lady fiddled nervously with her clipboard. 'The nurse looked at their hair before we set out.'

The grey face swung to Pauline. 'Have they got their ration books?'

The lady said, 'I've got them here.'

'Have they been told about wiping their boots?'

'Yes, Mrs Prosser,' lied Pauline.

'And about noise?'

'Yes, Mrs Prosser.'

'You've taken them up and shown them their beds?'

'Yes, Mrs Prosser.'

There was a pause, and the lady said, 'I'm sure they're going to be very comfortable.' She smiled at them. 'Aren't you?'

'We don't know yet,' said Jack.

A sound like the hiss of a serpent came from Mrs Prosser. There was a moment's silence and then the lady beside her started to make excuses, but the grey face leant back with the chin pulled in to the thin neck and the words fell silent. They heard the breath in Mrs Prosser's nostrils before she spoke.

'I want them out of my sight,' she said. 'At once.'

Pauline would not let them say a word until they had climbed to the top of the house.

'Oh,' she said, 'I'll just plonk meself down here till I get me breath back.' She sat in the single chair looking down into her lap and after a moment her shoulders began shaking. It was more than David could bear to see her sobbing and he went and stood in front of her, wanting to touch her but not daring. She looked up and her face was red, but not with tears. She was giggling. 'That young skite Jack,' she said. 'I don't know how he dare!'

David had made a mistake. He tried to grin, but knew there was too much alarm in his face and he tried to move away. Pauline reached and grasped his hand. 'No. Don't go away. Somebody's got to protect me from those two demons.'

'I only spoke the truth,' Jack protested. 'We don't know if we're going to like it yet.' He turned to Alec. 'Do we?'

Alec's pale brow was wrinkled. 'Her downstairs,' he said. 'If that's what *she's* like, what's going to happen when Mr Prosser comes home?'

'Oh hell,' said Jack. 'I hadn't thought.'

'Well you don't need to.' Pauline got to her feet. 'And don't let me hear you using language like that any more.'

'I only said hell.'

'That's enough!' She went briskly to the big wardrobe. 'You don't need worry about Mr Prosser coming home. He's dead.'

'Whew!' Jack let out his breath. 'That was a narrow squeak. I couldn't bear two like that.'

Pauline suddenly turned on him. 'That's just where you're wrong, clever clogs. He wasn't anything like the Missus. Never a bit. Mr Prosser was a lovely man. He was that gentle you felt you always wanted to talk to him, and,' her voice rose, 'I won't have a word said against him.'

Jack was taken aback, but only for a moment. 'But he married *her*,' he said.

Pauline sighed, and they could hear her mother and all the other village women talking as she said, 'It's such a shame they never had any children. But she never would, never in a million years. He wanted them, you could tell that. He was a bit shy like, even with lads and lasses, but he had such a lovely big kind face and eyes just like little Davey's here.' She was teasing now. 'He's going to be a lady-killer, aren't you, Davey?'

'I wish you'd shut up,' he said.

'Look, I've made him blush. But it is true, you have got nice big eyes.'

'What about mine?' said Jack.

'You! You're too cheeky by half. Yours are wicked,' and she turned to open the wardrobe door. 'Now here's where you've got to hang your clothes. There's plenty of room.'

'Smells of mothballs,' said Jack, 'and it looks as though somebody's already using it.'

'It's only just one old suit,' she said. 'You three don't look as though you're going to need much space.'

'Whose suit is it?'

Pauline turned to face them. 'It's Mr Prosser's, and I don't want you saying a word about it, any of you, or you'll get me the sack just as sure as night follows day. When he died she made me throw everything out. The lot. Every single thing that was his. I don't think she'd ever wanted him – not him, not children, nothing. All she wants is to sit in state and have the whole village think she's bliddy royalty.'

'Who's swearing now?'

Pauline had reddened. 'Well she makes you. And she wasn't going to have everything her own way, not if I had anything to do with it. So I kept his suit, the old one he wore every day. He used to keep sweets in the pockets for all us kiddies in the village.' She turned back to the open wardrobe. 'Anyway it's still his house and he has a right to be here.'

She reached to move the coat hanger along the rail and, as it slid, the suit swung round so that the back of the jacket was towards them. It was broad and gingery. David had seen it before.

The village school was smaller than the one they were used to, but not so very different. The coke stove had the same breathless fumes, and the blackboard chalk had the same dry taste when you put it on your tongue. Jack found new friends and fought with them in the playground, Alec felt the cold as the winter came on, and David tried to keep up with the big lads and not be homesick, but the ache was with him most of the time.

They hardly ever saw Mrs Prosser. She made sure of that. Once a day a woman came up from the village to cook lunch for her, but they had to stay at school and eat the sandwiches that Pauline made for them. And by the time school was over, and they climbed the hill and turned the corner, the house was bleak and dark and already closed down for the night. Except for the kitchen. They were not allowed to use the front door, and they would not have wanted to, because it was easier to get to the kitchen through the yard at the back, and they knew the fire would still be burning and Pauline waiting for them. David used to think it was like coming out of the dark into a secret burrow with the yellow light of the oil lamp in the centre of the table gleaming on the plates set out for them, and showing the steam curling from the kettle on the hob.

'Something hot,' said Pauline. 'You need it when the nights draw in.' Generally it was soup. 'I'm not the world's best cook,' she said, but she would roast potatoes at the edge of the fire, and bring bread her mother had baked and sent up to the house because 'couldn't bear the thought of young lads going to bed on an empty stomach'.

It was the best part of the day. They lived in the kitchen, and gradually it began to feel as though they had always been there. The two bigger boys tried to make it belong to them. They never quite succeeded.

They had not been there long when Jack said one night, 'Where's the wireless? I like that when I'm at home.'

Pauline shook her head. 'We haven't got electricity, and she won't have it in the house anyway.'

'What does she do, then?'

'She sews. She does beautiful embroidery.'

'Her?' He didn't believe it. 'I bet she catches beetles and eats them.'

Pauline laughed, but she hushed him and glanced at the door to the hall. 'You never quite know where she is,' she whispered. 'She moves so quiet.'

They were noisy enough most nights playing Ludo, which Pauline had brought from home, or they drew pictures, especially David, or sometimes Pauline read to them, mostly stories about murder and love from little books with grey pages she smuggled into the house.

But by seven o'clock the fire was only a few red coals in the grate, and it was time for her to go home and for them to go to bed. Every night she lit a candle and went ahead of them into the dark hall. They moved quietly in the silent house because boots were forbidden and the boys were in their socks. There was always a scuffle because nobody wanted to be last in line with the darkness creeping at their heels as they went higher, and David always lost until Pauline saw what was happening and made either Jack or Alec go alongside him – in case he stumbled, she said.

But still the great whispering well of the stairs surged around them, and the little light made tall shadows lean into walls and doorways and wait for them on the landings above.

'Be quick then,' she always said as she put the candlestick on the floor and left them as they got undressed. She had to come back, once they were in bed, and take the candle because Mrs Prosser would not allow it to be left. David was clumsy with his clothes, and often she had to help him on with his pyjama jacket, but it gave her the chance to tuck him in which she always wanted to do because he looked so small and forlorn.

The great whispering well of the stairs surged around them

'Sleep tight.' She would take one last look around the room and they would see the cracks of light fade around the edges of the door as her steps clattered down the bare stairs.

They huddled under their blankets, talking in the dark about home. David listened. He never said very much, but as the other two talked he walked with them from the lamp post where they always met at nights until the blackout came, and along the street until he saw his mother waiting, and then he realized that his eyes were wet, and his pillow was damp, and he curled tighter and screwed up a corner of the sheet until it was the shape of the limp toy dog he always took to bed at home. He had been afraid to bring it with him.

One night he was almost asleep when Alec said into the darkness, 'I wouldn't like to be left here alone. I bet there's ghosts.'

'Don't be daft,' said Jack. 'Who needs ghosts when we've got her downstairs?'

'But I bet there is. I bet David thinks there is.'

They asked him. He hardly heard them because he had the sheet to his lips and was far away. Alec insisted. 'Are there any ghosts in this house, David?'

'I don't know,' he said, but the thought of the man on the landing drifted into his mind. He let it fade. It was too long ago and too misty, and he did not want the misery of that day to come back. 'I don't know.'

'You're hopeless you are. Anyway,' Alec turned over with a lot of noise, 'nothing would ever make me stay here by meself.'

'Nor me,' said Jack. 'Never.'

Christmas was a few days away and it brought an excitement that had nothing to do with parcels and presents. Christmas cards came from Newcastle with letters tucked inside from mothers saying that as there had been no raids for quite a while it was safe to come home for a short time. Everybody's cheeks seemed to be glowing with the same good news.

'And me Dad's on leave,' Jack shouted in the kitchen. 'Man, it's going to be great!'

Alec had a letter saying he was to catch the same bus as Jack, but David's letter was slow coming. It was the day before Christmas Eve, and Jack and Alec were already packed ready to leave that afternoon, when the post came with David's letter. They all crowded round to find out when he was leaving.

It was Pauline who told her mother what had happened. 'His little fingers were that clumsy he could hardly get it out of the envelope. Just like a baby he looks sometimes. And there was a letter and a postal order. "That'll be for your fare home," said one of the lads, but Davey was reading what his Mam said. I've never seen a look on a boy's face quite like I seen then. It was a lovely letter, I read it, but his Mam told him she didn't think it was safe and that he wasn't going to go home after all. I had to turn me back. The look in that little lad's eyes was something I never want to see again.'

David did not cry. Jack, watching him carefully, said, 'You're a good lad, Davey,' and then he and Alec whispered in the corner, and Pauline heard the chink of pennies. When they put on their coats and boots and went out secretively she knew that they were going down to the shop to buy him a present before their bus left. It was all they could do to cheer him up.

To prevent her own tears welling up again Pauline said, 'That's a pretty card your Mam sent, Davey. Nice little red robin.' He nodded. It was a tiny card, very small, like his mother. 'But I don't believe you've sent one to her.'

'I did.'

'But not a proper one. Not one you made yourself. Anyone can send an old bought card.'

She knew he liked drawing. 'Tell you what,' she said as she led him to the window, 'see that old tree behind the yard? It's still got some lovely leaves on it, all red and yellow. Why don't you go and get some while I get a big piece of paper and make some flour paste, and then you can stick them on to your picture and send them to your Mam. There's still time; it's not Christmas Eve till tomorrow.'

She watched him cross the yard and then she smoothed her dress and bit her lips. His letter had been bad news for her, too, and the bell that suddenly rang meant that she had to face up to it.

Mrs Prosser's few Christmas cards were of the dark kind, and they stood among the black ornaments on the mantel as a reminder that Christmas was midwinter and cold and hard. Pauline felt their chill as she told Mrs Prosser that not all the boys were leaving for the holiday.

'Why's that? Has his mother no feeling?' The thin voice did not wait for an explanation. 'These people ought never to have children. They can't wait to saddle other people with them.' She waved Pauline away. 'Get the other two ready. I can't wait to see the back of them.'

Pauline fled. For the next hour there was bustle, and when Jack and Alec had given her David's present to hide, she went with them down to the village to make sure they caught the bus.

David was alone in the kitchen. All he could do now was to pretend. He pretended he was going home and he had to hurry to finish the big Christmas card he was making for his mother. He was drawing on the sheet of paper Pauline had given him when he heard the door to the hall open. He did not want to look up, but he slowly raised his eyes. Mrs Prosser stood there with her monkey fingers clasped in front of her black dress.

For a long moment neither moved, then her voice snapped at him, 'Stand up!' He slid off his chair. 'Stand up when a lady comes into the room!'

She swished forward so smoothly she seemed not to have legs under her long dress. 'So you're the one that's staying.' He saw her lips had bluish blisters. 'Your mother expects me to provide your Christmas dinner, I suppose. Oh does she, indeed!' Her breath hissed as she sucked it in. 'There will be no heathen feast in this house. No Christmas dinner, so don't expect it. The very idea!'

Indignation raged inside her, and she was turning away when quite suddenly she stopped. Her chin was pulled in so tightly it seemed to be part of her neck, and she was looking down at the table. 'What on earth is that?'

The red leaves were spread out in front of him, and for the first time David had a question he could answer. 'I'm going to stick them on a picture for me Mam.'

His voice was no more than a murmur, and her action was equally silent. She leant forward and scraped the leaves into one bony hand, crunched them like waste paper, and threw them into the back of the fire.

'That for your mother!' she said. 'I will not have my kitchen made into a Newcastle slum.' The door slammed.

When Pauline came back, David's picture was also on the fire. 'I didn't feel like doing it,' he said. He wanted to cry but he did not dare, and she did not question him.

She gave him all his favourite things for tea, and stayed with him late, reading a story to him as he lay in bed, something she had never done when the others were there.

When she tucked him in she whispered, 'I'll leave you the candle, Davey, but don't let on to the Missus.'

At the door she turned and smiled at him, then the latch dropped. He heard her footsteps on the stair, another door opened and closed, and he was in a silence so deep he thought he heard the flutter of the candle flame.

He lay as she had left him, curled up on his side, looking at Alec's empty bed. Behind him, Jack's bed would be the same – flat and empty. He was alone in the long room, and the frosty night crept in and held the candle flame stiff – as smooth as an almond. No sound, and all that emptiness at his back.

He turned his head on the pillow until he could see the wardrobe towering against the wall. From where he lay the long mirrors of its doors were blank, but the columns on either side shone in the candle flame as though they guarded a yawning gateway.

Then deep inside it something moved, and at the same instant a voice from almost alongside him dragged him round. The door to the stairs was open and the tall figure of Mrs Prosser was in the room. She made no noise. It was her reflection he had seen in the mirror.

'I knew it!' Her voice was as bitter as the icy air as she swept to the foot of his bed and pointed at the candle. 'Who gave you this?'

Words did not come. From his pillow he looked up at her. In the candlelight the blue flecks on her lips were black.

'Am I going to wait all night for an answer?'

The pointing hand suddenly clenched and he drew himself into a ball, ready for her to reach over and strike. But the blow did not come. Her hand came down, and something that may have been a smile pushed at her wrinkles. Even her voice was softer.

'But I don't suppose you like being on your own, do you, sonny?' He shook his head. 'And I suppose you are afraid of the dark.' He nodded. 'Very, very afraid, I expect.'

He watched the wrinkles at the corner of her mouth deepen, and now she was definitely smiling. 'After all,' she said, 'it's almost Christmas.'

He tried to smile.

'Well,' she said, and her voice was still soft, 'you know you deserve a thrashing, don't you?' She waited for his nod. He had to give it. 'Worse than a thrashing in fact.' Her voice rose. 'And worse than a thrashing you shall have!'

As she spoke she snatched at the candle and turned for the door. 'You will stay in this room all night and all tomorrow until I tell you to come out!'

The flame streamed and dipped in front of her as she swept out. The door closed with a bang, and then the next, but even before he heard it slam he had scrabbled at the bedclothes and pulled them tight around himself as he crouched.

He heard himself sob, but the echo made the black room emptier and he stifled the sound. The sheets seemed clammy, as though they were never intended to be laid over a living creature, and his shivers made the iron bedstead give out little sounds like beetles' feet until he clamped his arms around his knees and controlled the trembling.

He heard a night bird shriek briefly on the hillside above the house, and then it, too, was swallowed in the silence of the night and everything was utterly still. He could not hear even the sound of his own breathing, but as his eyes stared into the darkness, and the silence in the room became more dense, he gradually saw the shape of the window against the stars.

It was then, in the corner beyond the foot of the bed, that he heard something shift. His bones were rigid, as cold as iron. He was clamped motionless.

Silence. His breath crept into his mouth. Then the sound came again. His eyes were as wide as an owl's, and in the starlight he saw the wardrobe door sigh open.

He flung himself across the empty bed, and his feet were on cold lino as his fingers fumbled for the latch. It bit his fingers, but the door was open and he plunged into the blackness of the stairs. His foot missed the tread. He clutched for the handrail but missed it and fell, twisting in the rushing darkness until his shoulder and back crashed into the door at the bottom. The catch burst and he fell out on to the bare boards of the landing.

There was a glimmer of light downstairs. Mrs Prosser had stopped and was looking up. Her face halted him. The candle, gleaming like a star, made her mouth a pitiless shadow and her eyes two dark pits. But he had to go down to escape from whatever had swung the wardrobe door. He was too late. Something large and dark moved out from the burst doorway and brushed past him. He could see it against the whitewashed wall; the shape of a man, blocking his way.

David shrank. He was no more than a fistful of fear, and the man looked down at him. In the faint light from below, the man's face was hardly visible. It was no more than a blur of heavy moustache and eyebrows, which threw a deep shadow over its eyes, but David felt their gaze and his blood slowed, and the silence stiffened until it seemed nothing would move again.

It was then that the figure turned away. He watched it as it began to descend, seeming to tread heavily, but no sound came. The well of the stairs was a column of silence, with the spark of the candle shining faintly. Mrs Prosser's head was still tilted upwards. She saw what was coming, and the candle trembled, but she did not move. Fear held her motionless until it was too late.

The figure of the man was only two steps above her when, in a sudden stab of terror, she thrust the candle at him as though to scorch him out of the air. But his big hand reached and closed over hers. It was then that she cried out and began to struggle. She could not save herself. The candle flared, fell and went out.

As darkness engulfed the whole staircase, David ran down into it, sliding his hand down the banister. Nothing would keep him alone at the top of the house.

He heard Mrs Prosser fall. She did not cry out or even moan. He heard the thud of her arms, hips and head on the stairs, a soft slither, then silence.

He remembered the sole of his foot treading on something warm that yielded beneath it, but then he was over it and crossing the cold floor of the kitchen to the back door.

His mother came that day, not to fetch him but to stay that night and the next, over Christmas. They were in Pauline's house down in the village with the stream outside the door, where she had found him standing on the ice.

'I don't know how we are ever going to thank you,' said his mother for the tenth time. She was still shy, sitting very upright in the easy chair by the big fire as Pauline bustled about fetching tea. 'It was such a terrible shock when I got your message.'

Pauline's mother, round-cheeked like her daughter, smiled. 'Now just you put your mind at rest. Davey stays with us from now on. He could hardly go back there, could he?'

The two women looked at each other. They understood one another. David, in the warmth of the fire with the tinsel of the Christmas tree trembling at his elbow, bowed his head over the drawing pad on his knee and pretended he was not listening as all three lowered their voices.

'Poor soul. What a terrible way to go.'

'And that little lad in the house all on his own. He hasn't said much about it, and I don't like to ask.'

Pauline glanced at him, and he started to hum to himself and bent further over his drawing. She turned her back to him and lowered her voice even further. 'She must have been up in his room. Must have been. I'm just sure one of those boys told her what was up there, because she had it with her when we found her at the foot of the stairs. It must have been the last thing she saw before she died.'

David's mother did not understand.

'Mr Prosser's old suit,' said Pauline. 'It was wrapped around her. Tight. Really tight.'

David's picture had a house standing in the snow, and you could see firelight through the windows. He would give it to his mother in the morning.

The Deadfall
Ted Hughes

I own a tiny ivory fox about an inch and a half long. Most likely an Eskimo carving. It came to me in one of the strangest incidents of my life.

My mother saw ghosts, now and again. Different kinds. One night during the last war she woke, feeling dreadfully agitated. She lay for a while, feeling more and more agitated. At last she got out of bed and, opening the curtains, saw an amazing sight. Across the street stood St George's Church. And above the church, the whole sky was throbbing with flashing crosses. As she told of it next day, there were thousands on thousands, flashing and fading, in and out, the whole sky covered with them, coming very thick, like big snowflakes hitting and breaking and melting on a warm window. She tried to wake my father. 'There's the most terrible battle somewhere,' she told him. 'Thousands of boys are being killed.' He heard what she said, but he wouldn't be roused. He had to get up at five a.m. anyway, as every morning. She went back to the window and watched for a long time, going to bed finally only when she got too cold.

Next day, the radio announced that the British and American armies had landed that night in Northern

France, and were fighting their way inland through the German defences.

Another time, she was awakened by a sickening pain across the back of her neck and a terrific banging. Short, urgent bursts of banging, as if somebody were pounding hard on a door or hammering on a table. She couldn't tell where the noise came from. 'It shook this house,' she said. Again she got up and looked out of the window. But the street, which was the main street of the town, was deserted. She went downstairs, made herself a cup of tea, and sat with the pain. It felt, she said, like toothache – but in her neck. She couldn't tell how the banging stopped – eventually it just wasn't there any more. But she still had the pain next morning when the telegram came with the news of the violent death, during the night, of one of her brothers.

She was ready for this news. She had known somebody in her family was going to die. And the moment she read the telegram the pain went.

Another time, while she was pushing a Hoover around the sitting room, mid-afternoon, her eldest brother walked in. She was alarmed, since she knew that he was actually lying unable to move in Halifax hospital. As she switched off the Hoover to speak to him, he faded. She noted the time, guessing he had died that very moment. Again, she had known that one of her family was going to die.

Each time, she was warned in the same way. Among her seven or eight brothers and sisters, as a girl her closest friend had been the sister closest to her in age, Miriam. This sister died when both were in their late teens. A few months after her death, Miriam reappeared at night and sat on my mother's bed, just as in life, and held her hand. Without speaking, she seemed to be consoling my mother. Two days later, their baby brother died.

After that, through the years, just before any member of her family died, Miriam would appear at my mother's bedside. But as the years passed, her ghost changed. She became brighter and taller. 'Gradually,' said my mother, 'she has turned into an angel.' By the time of that last occasion, when their eldest brother died, Miriam had become a tall glowing angel with folded wings. My mother described her as being made of flame. As if she were covered with many-coloured feathers of soft, pouring flame. But it was still Miriam. And on this last visit, as she stood by the bed, my mother reached up to stroke the flame because it was, as she said, 'so beautiful'. 'The feel of it,' she told us afterwards, 'was like the taste of honey.' I remember her telling that, the next day, as if it were minutes ago.

My brother and sister and I also wanted to see ghosts.

We lived near Hebden Bridge, in West Yorkshire, in a village called Mytholmroyd. There the river runs in a deep valley, under high horizons of empty moorland. On one side of that valley, in a steep wood of oak and birch trees, is an ancient grave. At least, it was always known as a grave. We called it the grave of the ancient Briton. A great rough slab of stone. My brother, much older than myself, sometimes tried to dig him up, with the help of a few friends. I remember scraping away there, on two or three occasions. The stone was embedded in a hole and far too big for us to lever out. We tried to dig round it and under it. But the great slab simply settled deeper.

My brother liked to camp out on the hillsides, and would take me with him. Once, when he and I were camping down by the stream in that wood, not far from the grave, he got the idea of raising the ancient Briton's ghost.

He must have already thought about it quite carefully, because he was prepared. Perhaps not very well prepared. He had brought half a bottle of sweet wine made from blackberries. One of our uncles concocted that sort of thing. This was to work the magic trick.

He woke me in the middle of the night. I pulled on my boots and climbed through the woods behind him. I liked being in the woods at night, but by the time we got to the grave I was nervous. I remember I didn't want him to go too near the grave. I thought something might grab him and pull him in. Then I would be alone, in a dark wood, with my brother somewhere beneath me being dragged deeper into the earth. I didn't like that idea.

He had already made what he called the altar – a flat piece of stone near the grave's edge. Now he lit a fire on this stone. I saw he had firewood ready. In his pre- parations he had even emptied the charge out of some twelve-bore cartridges, to make sure he got an instant flare-up blaze, by lighting the loose explosive. That bit was a success. It lit up the tree trunks and the over-curving boughs in a great woosh of light, as if they'd flung up their arms. Then it settled down to burn the twigs he'd piled in a wigwam shape. He was an expert firemaker and in no time had a good blaze going.

Now he stood up with his bottle of wine and carefully tipped it, letting a trickle spatter into the flames. The glow blackened and hissed, as a great cloud billowed up. He began to speak:

'O ancient Briton, I am pouring out this redness to give life to you. Rise up, O ancient Briton, all this is for you. Rise up and warm yourself. Rise up, O ancient Briton, and quench your ancient thirst.'

I remember that 'quench your ancient thirst', because that was the first time I ever felt the sensation of my hair going freezingly cold, like a cap of solid ice. And I was suddenly afraid. I could see the ancient Briton, deep in the earth, with his corpse teeth bared. Probably his eyes had just flown open. I just knew he would come – and he wouldn't know what to do about it. What could my brother do, when that thing started walking towards us?

My brother was already backing towards me, as if he'd seen something down there in the pit where the stone lay. As he came, he was still trickling wine out on to the tough, leathery grass of the wood. Then he set the bottle down, half-leaning, still with some wine in it, halfway between me and the fire, and joined me. The fire had recovered, the blackberry wine seemed to have helped it.

Perhaps he did other things that I hadn't noticed. We watched the flames and the huge caves of blackness between the tree trunks. Little sparks went writhing up in the reddened smoke. I stared hard, to see a shape beyond them. I kept an eye on the bottle.

I expected something. Maybe a dark lump like an animal would heave itself up out of the hole. Or maybe a person would somehow be there, standing beside the grave, looking towards us.

Or maybe we wouldn't see anything, but the bottle

would suddenly rise up in the air and tilt, as an invisible mouth drank at it. Then a shape would grow solid between us and the fire, with the bottle in its hand.

But the worst thought was, if something did come what would we do?

We crouched there, watching the fire till the flames died.

I asked in a whisper if he thought we should go back to the tent, but he hissed so sharp and tense I felt the hair prickle all over my body. He was staring towards the glow of the fire's embers. I tried to see what he was looking at.

'I thought I saw something,' he whispered.

I began to hear sounds in the wood, rustling and tickings. I felt sleepy. Surely the fire had gone out now. He got up at last and walked over to it. I followed him, to stay close. He picked up the bottle and poured the last drops on to the fire's remains. He turned the altar over with his foot. Nothing had happened.

My little ivory fox came the following summer. This time we were camping in the valley known as Crimsworth Dene.

Our father and mother had both been born in Hebden Bridge. Their paradise had been the deep, cliffy, dead-end gorge of Hardcastle Crags, which cuts back north-west into the moors from Hebden Bridge, full of trees, with a rocky river. The big old mill building still standing there, well up the gorge, was used as a dance hall in those days, where all the boys and girls of Hebden Bridge did their courting. Nowadays, this place is a famous beauty spot. More than once, people from Hebden Bridge, on holiday in Blackpool or Morecambe, have purchased a bus ticket for a day's mystery tour to a beauty spot, and have been brought back to Hardcastle Crags.

Crimsworth Dene is a more secret valley that forks away due north, from the bottom of Hardcastle Crags.

Like all these valleys, Crimsworth Dene is steep-sided, deep, with woods overhanging stone-walled, falling-away fields. And above the woods, more stone-walled fields, climbing to a farm or two. And above the farms the moors – the empty prairies of heather that roll away north into Scotland. And in the very bottom of the valley, the dark, deep cleft, thick with beech, oak, sycamore, plunging to an invisible stream.

On the west slope, an old stony packhorse road clambers north between drystone walls, under the hanging woods and above the lower fields, finally up and out across the moor towards Haworth. About a mile up that road, on the left, over the roadway, is a little level clearing.

Perhaps it was once a quarry, for the stone of the local walls. Here, when they were boys, before the First World War, my mother's brothers used to camp. They called Crimsworth Dene 'the happy valley'. The strangest thing that ever happened to me happened there.

One week, my brother decided to camp there. Though it was right in the heart of the territory that belonged, as I felt, to our mother and father, it was a little outside ours. But our uncles knew the farmers, and they had given my brother permission to shoot rabbits and magpies and such like. Now and again he did roam this far with his rifle, but only rarely and briefly. For me, though I had always known Hardcastle Crags, it was the first time I had ever entered Crimsworth Dene. I was still quite young, only seven.

As we pitched our tent on the Friday evening, on that little clearing, under the trees, I knew this was the most magical place I had ever been in. The air was very still, and the sky clear after a warm day. All down the valley, over the great spilling mounds of foxgloves, grey columns of midges hung in the stillness, like vertical smoke above camp-fires. I brought water up from the stream in our rope-handled canvas bucket, and collected dead sticks for firewood, while he sorted our bedding, the pans and cutlery, and made a fireplace with stones. All the while a bird sang on the very topmost twig of a tree over the clearing. I had never heard a bird like it, nor have I since.

It was a thrush, I expect. But every note echoed through the whole valley. I felt I had to talk in whispers. Even so, I thought each word we spoke would be heard in Pecket, away out of sight round the hill's shoulder, a mile or more away.

My brother got a fire going and warmed up our beans. Camping is mainly about camp-fires, food cooked on camp-fires, and going to sleep in a tent. And getting up in the wet dawn. We planned to get up at dawn, maybe before dawn, when the rabbits would be dopy, bobbing about in the long dewy grass. Our precious, beautiful thing, my brother's gleaming American rifle, lay in the tent, on a blanket.

As it grew dark, I kept hearing a tune in my head and the words of the song. It came to me whenever I looked down over the deep grass of the steep field below us towards that plunge of dark trees. Very clear I heard:

If you go down to the woods today
You're sure of a big surprise

and the strange tune of that song, which sounds like a bear romping through a gloomy forest.

As I lay on my groundsheet, under my blanket at last, looking up at the taut canvas of our bell-tent, and listening to the stars, and the huge, silent breathing of the valley, I felt happier than I had ever been. And wider awake than I had ever been. Even so, I went straight off to sleep.

I woke in the dark, thinking it must be time to get up. I lay listening for night creatures. After a long time I began to hear cockcrows, then the tent walls began to pale. My brother woke and, without breakfast, we were off.

Dark tracks of rabbits were everywhere in the white of the heavy dew. I looked at the tracks quite close around our tent. Why hadn't I heard whatever made them? What had made them? Rabbits, or something else?

Usually, one rabbit was all we could expect to shoot. But because this was new hunting ground, and because the place seemed so magically wild, secret and undisturbed, I was hoping for a record bag. We saw hardly a rabbit. Only the odd white tail far off, just glimpsed then gone. The sun rose. The dew glittered and dried. We tramped all over the hillside, up as far as the moor. We skulked along the edges of woods, peering over walls. We had to inspect every tiny thing. It might be a snipe. Or the lifted head of a grouse strayed down off the high ground. But my brother did not fire one shot. For the last part of the morning we stretched out in the heather and he sunbathed.

But then, coming back to our camp for breakfast at midday, we found something curious. The wall along the top of the wood, directly above our camp, had a tumbledown gap. As we came down through that gap, my brother pointed.

Under the wall, on the wood side, a big flat stone like a flagstone, big as a gravestone, leaned outwards, on end. It was supported, I saw, by a man-made contraption of slender sticks. Tucked in behind the sticks, under the leaning slab, lay a dead woodpigeon, its breast torn, showing the dark meat.

'Gamekeeper's deadfall,' said my brother.

It was the first deadfall I had seen set. I had read about them, made of massive tree trunks, used by trappers in the Canadian forests for bears, wolves, wolverines. My brother explained how it worked. How one light touch on the tripstick would collapse the support and bring the great stone slam down flat – on top of whatever was under it.

I went past it warily. I didn't want the jolt of my tread to bring it down.

'The pigeon is fresh,' said my brother. 'He must have baited it yesterday. Or maybe this morning. For a fox, probably.'

We hadn't seen the gamekeeper, who looked after Lord Savile's grouse up on the moor. He only became a danger if you'd shot some of his grouse and this time we hadn't. Still, we'd kept a sharp lookout for him.

A gamekeeper usually sees you first. And the moment he sees you, he becomes invisible – till he's right on top of you.

In the afternoon, we went back up on to the heather. My brother was mad about sunbathing. He rubbed himself with olive oil and lay there frying. I lay for a while. But I wasn't mad about the sun. I left that to him. Eventually, I found a trickle of water that overflowed an old drinking trough and spent the afternoon making dams and channels.

Rabbits usually come out again about four o'clock. But still we had no luck. Somehow, in spite of all the tracks in the dew, and in spite of the silent, lonely emptiness of the valley, rabbits seemed to know better than to show themselves in the day. We ended up drinking tea at a farmhouse, where the farmer said his old mother, who made the tea then sat watching us from a rocking chair in the corner, was some remote cousin of our grandmother. After that, he wanted us to shoot a particular rat. This rat was stealing eggs, according to him. Its front doorway was a crevice under the threshold of an old stable. Every evening he saw it. But it was far too smart to be trapped. He gave us two addled eggs that we propped up, very visible, three yards in front of its hole. Then we climbed to a hayloft, and lay looking down at both eggs and rat-hole, through the open loft door.

We lay there unmoving, on the warm boards, with our eyes on that hole, till the light began to fail. Maybe the rat was watching us from inside his hole. He never appeared. I became impatient, thinking of the rabbits we were missing. They were probably out all over the place. I wanted to take home at least one.

Finally, my brother gave in and we went back down over the fields from the high farm, to our camp. We saw rabbits, but it was too dark now to see the sights of the rifle. Anyway, I found I was more interested in getting to the gap in the wall. I couldn't wait to see the trap. I imagined a great red fox in it, squashed flat. Or maybe a stoat. A stoat would easily trip those frail, balanced sticks. Or maybe even a crow. A stoat might leap clear.

But it yawned there just as we'd left it, and the woodpigeon lay untouched.

My idea of the valley was changing. I had thought of it teeming with stoats, weasels, foxes – as well as rabbits. But here, as everywhere else, perhaps the gamekeepers and the poultry farmers were in control. Even crows. I hadn't seen a crow. I hadn't seen a magpie. A magpie would have found that woodpigeon anywhere in the valley.

But the gamekeeper had set the trap, so there must be something. Maybe, as my brother said, there was a fox. A lone fox, a notorious, solitary bandit, with his hide-out in this wood, near our camp. Among rocks, maybe, where he couldn't be dug out. And maybe tomorrow morning he'd be there, flat under the fallen slab. Or she. It might be a vixen.

The evening was as still as the night before. As we fried eggs and bacon, and our pork and beans to go with them, the magical spell came over me again. The thought of a fox very near, deep in his den, maybe smelling our bacon, made everything more mysterious. I kept looking down through the dusk into the crevasse of dark trees below, to give myself the eerie feeling of that tune again, and the strange words:

If you go down to the woods today
You're sure of a big surprise . . .

It never failed. As the valley grew darker, the feeling,

with its bear coming up through the forest, grew even stronger. Whenever I looked down there, and thought of that tune, I found I could make myself shiver and freeze afresh. Like touching myself with an electric spark. I kept testing myself to see if it would go on happening. And every time it happened.

The fox would be smelling our bacon all right, and our coffee. We always brewed coffee in the dusk. That was the part I liked best of all, sitting there, gazing into the fire and sipping sweet, scalding coffee, while the thick sticks crumbled to a cave of glow, whitening the hearthstones. Maybe those tracks in the dew last night had been the fox, inspecting us and our fireplace and looking for leftovers.

Again we planned to get up early. Some time tomorrow, Sunday, we would have to set off back home. My brother wanted to bag something as badly as I did. He was regretting wasting time on the rat.

That night I tried to stay awake, so I could have every minute of lying there under my blanket, listening. Each tiny sound had to be something. I could hear the stream, down in the bottom. Why hadn't I heard that the night before? Would I hear a fox if he came right up to the tent wall, and sniffed at me through the canvas?

At some point I drifted off to sleep because when I woke I thought it was dawn. Then I realized, the pale light coming through the canvas was moonlight. I was absolutely alert, and tense. Something had wakened me. I lay there, hardly daring to breathe. Then I heard a whisper, a low hiss of a whisper, outside the tent. It was calling my name.

Somebody was out there. My brother was breathing gently beside me, fast asleep. I simply listened. I don't know what I thought. I felt no fear, but still I was amazed to feel the tears trickling slowly down over my ears, as I lay staring upwards.

The whisper came again, my name. It seemed to be coming from about where the fire was.

Very carefully, partly not to waken my brother, partly not to let the voice know I was listening, I sat up, leaned forward, and tried to peep through the laced-up door of the tent. By holding the edges of the flaps slightly apart, I could see a tiny dot of red glow still in our fireplace. Everything out there was drenched in a grey, misty light.

Somebody was standing beside the fireplace.

It was a person and yet I got the impression it was somehow not a person. Or it was a very small person. It looked like a small old woman, with a peculiar bonnet on her head and a long shawl. That was my impression. As I stared with all my might, trying to make out something definite, this figure drifted backwards into the shade of the trees. But the whisper came again:

'Come out. Quickly. There's been an accident.'

I immediately knew it must be somebody from the farm. Surely it was the farmer's little old mother. That was how she knew we were here. The farmer had fallen down a well, or down a loft ladder, or a mad, calving cow had gored him and crushed his ribs. Or he'd simply tumbled downstairs going to get his old mother a cup of tea because she couldn't sleep.

Something stopped me waking my brother. What I really wanted was to find out more. Who was this person? What was the accident? Anyway, it was my name that had been called. It must be me that was specially needed. I could come back and tell my brother later. Most of all, I wanted to see who this was.

I had gone to sleep in my clothes, to keep warm and for a quick start. So now I pulled on my boots. I unlaced the tent door at the bottom and crawled out. The grass was cold and soaking under my hands.

'Hurry,' came the whisper from under the trees. 'Hurry, hurry.'

It seems strange, that I felt no fear. I was so sure that it was somebody from the farm, that I thought of no other possibility. Only huge curiosity, and excitement. Also, I felt quite important suddenly.

I went toward the voice, staring into the dark shade. The moon was past full but very hard and white. I wanted to get into the shade quickly, where I wouldn't be so visible.

But now the voice came again, from further up the wood. Yes, the voice was climbing towards the farm.

'Hurry,' it kept saying. 'Hurry up.'

Beneath the trees, the slope was clear and grassy, without brambles or undergrowth. Easy going but steep, with that tough, slippery grass.

As I climbed, the voice went ahead. Very soon, I could see through the top of the wood. The bright night sky was piled with brilliant masses of snowy cloud, beyond the dark tree stems. I glimpsed the black silhouette now and again, the funny bonnet, climbing ahead, bobbing between the trees.

'Are you coming?' came the whisper again. 'This way.'

I saw her shape in the gap of the wall, clear against those snowy clouds. Then she had gone through it. It was now, as I came up towards the gap, sometimes

I saw her shape in the gap of the wall, clear against those snowy clouds

grasping tussocks to help myself upwards, that I saw something else, bouncing and scrabbling under the wall, in a clear patch of moonlight.

At first I thought it was a rabbit, just this moment scared into a snare by our approach, now leaping and flinging itself to be free, but tethered by the pegged snare. It was the size of a rabbit. Then I smelt the rich, powerful smell.

With a shock, I remembered. I had come right up to the deadfall.

The great slab of stone had fallen. Beside it sat a well-grown fox cub, staring up at me, panting. As I took this in, the cub suddenly started again, tugging and bouncing, jerking and scrabbling, without a sound, till again it crouched there, staring up at me, its mouth wide open, its tongue dangling, panting.

I could see now that it was trapped by one hind leg and its tail. They were pinned to the ground under the corner of the big slab.

The smell was overpowering, thick, choking, almost liquid, as if concentrated liquid scent had been poured over me, saturating my clothes and hands. I knew the smell of fox – the overpowering smell of frightened fox.

Then I looked up and saw the figure out there in the field, only five yards away, watching me. More than ever I could see it was a little old woman, with her very thin legs and her funny bonnet and shawl. She did not seem to be wanting me to go to the farm. She had brought me to this fox cub. She was probably some eccentric old lady who never slept, or slept only by day and spent the night roaming the hillsides, talking to owls and befriending foxes. She would have seen our camp. Probably some of those tracks had been hers, brushed through the dew around our tent. Now she had found the trapped cub, and not being strong enough to lift the slab, she had come to us. She wanted me to lift the slab and free the cub. She had not called my brother because she thought he might kill it. She must have watched us, and heard him speak my name.

My first thought was to catch the cub and keep it alive. But how could I hold it and at the same time lift the slab? It was a desperate, ferocious little thing. I could have wrapped it in my jersey, knotting the arms round it. But I didn't think of that. As I put my fingers under the other corner of the slab, the cub snapped its teeth at me and hissed like a cat, then struggled again, jerking to free itself.

With all my strength I was just able to budge the slab a fraction. But it was enough. As the slab shifted, the cub scrabbled and was gone – off down the wood like a rocket.

I looked up at the old lady, and this was my next surprise. The bare, close-cropped, moonlit field was empty. I walked out to where she had been. The whole wide field, under the great bare sky of moonlight, all made much brighter by that great bulging heap of snowy, silvery clouds, was empty. Not even a sheep. Absolutely nothing.

She couldn't have run away. I had looked down for only a few seconds. She had simply gone. I could see every blade of grass where she had stood. The field wall. The trees of the wood. The hilltops above and beyond.

I came back to the deadfall. Now I saw that it lay at a slight tilt. There was something beneath it. Another cub, maybe. I tried again to lift it. But I still could not budge it more than that quarter inch, and only for a second. I could not possibly lift it.

It was as I came back down to our campsite that I saw somebody standing outside the tent, in the moonlight. I stopped, hidden under the trees. With a sudden terrible thought, I remembered the ancient Briton. And now, for the first time, I was really frightened.

But then I heard my name called in a familiar low voice. It was my brother. He had come out of the tent. And now he had heard me.

'Where have you been?'

I told him what had happened. All he said was, 'We'll have a look in the morning. Come and get back to sleep.'

But I lay awake. The tent darkened and became pitch black. Either the moon had gone down or that cloud had come up and covered it. Then I heard the prickling sound of light rain on the canvas.

The rain grew heavier, and soon it was filling the whole world, like a steady tearing of canvas inside my head. A drop hit my face.

Slowly the canvas paled. I heard cocks crowing in the high farms and dozed off. Next thing I smelt bacon. The rain had stopped. It was day.

'Come on, let's eat everything,' called my brother.

I wanted to see the deadfall, but he would not be hurried. We scoured our pans and dishes with grit and water and bundled them into their bag. He began to take down the wet tent. In a few minutes everything was inside a bulging kitbag. The rain had come back by now, but more of a drizzle. It looked to be setting in for the day. The shooting trip was over, I could see.

But now he took his rifle from under the tree where

he'd leaned it in the dry with the bag over its muzzle, and started off up the wood.

The deadfall lay as I had left it. He handed the rifle to me, put his fingers under the slab and heaved it back against the wall.

There, at our feet lay a big red fox, quite dead, the woodpigeon still in its mouth.

He pulled it clear and inspected it. The body was stiff. He picked it up by one hind leg. A foreleg stuck out at an angle. Its head was twisted to one side, keeping its grip on the dead bird. Only the tail plumed over, like a fern. I had expected to see whatever was under there flattened like a rat on the road. It did look slightly flattened, its fur was flattened.

Still carrying the dead animal by the one hind leg, my brother took the rifle from me and started off down the wood. But then he turned back, handed me the rifle again, and pulled the deadfall slab over. It dropped with a shocking thud into its position. I felt the earth bounce.

'This fox escaped,' he said.

Down at our campsite, he brought out our little axe. I asked him what we were going to do with the fox. Wasn't it the gamekeeper's? I remember his answer:

'This fox belongs to itself.'

Then he began to dig a hole with the axe in the middle of the patch of grass flattened by our tent. He cut out the turf and set it aside, then hacked down-wards, scooping the loosened soil out with his hands, till he began to hit stones. The hole was about two feet deep. He jabbed about down there with a sharpened stick, dislodging stones, and shaping the bottom of the hole. I crouched beside the work, watching the hole and looking at the fox. I had never examined a fox. It was so astonishing to see it there, so real, so near. When I lifted its eyelid, the eye looked at me, very bright and alive. I closed it gently, and stroked it quite shut. Its face was slightly squashed-looking, but with no visible damage, no blood. And so peculiar, with the woodpigeon gripped in its mouth.

My brother picked it up again.

'Do you want its tail?' he asked me. I shook my head.

He fitted it neatly into the bottom of the hole, and arranged it, bending the stiff, jutting foreleg to look more comfortable. We tucked the little stones around it, and covered it with the gritty black soil. Then the turfs. He took out some of the soil and threw it away, to let the turfs lie flat. I helped him push loose soil out of sight down between the sliced turfs. As I was doing this, I felt a knobbly pebble and saw under my fingers what looked like one of those white quartz pebbles you find embedded in the black boulders on the moor. But then I realized it was not a pebble.

I stood up to examine it. I could not believe what I had in my hand. It was this little ivory fox. I was so startled that I simply gripped it. Maybe I thought my brother might take it off me.

'What's wrong?' he asked, looking up. He never missed anything. But I managed to shift my inspection to the back of my fingers. I got my find into my pocket and bent again to the grave. He was combing the grass of the turfs with his fingers, drawing it over the edges, to make it look like unbroken sod again.

When he'd finished, you couldn't really tell it was there, even from quite close. Everything looked like the scuffed and trampled patch where a tent has been. As I stood there, I could feel him watching me. 'Are you all right?' he asked.

We had to walk down into Hebden Bridge, in the drizzle, to catch a bus home. He carried the kit bag, I carried the rifle. He had not fired one shot.

It was while we were waiting at the bus stop that he asked me who I thought the old woman was last night. Well, I said, it must have been just some old woman.

'But you said she vanished.'

'She did. One second she was there, and the next she wasn't.'

'Do you think,' he said, 'it might have been the dead fox's ghost?'

So it was there, standing at the bus stop in Hebden Bridge, that I first had to wonder whether I had seen a ghost. I didn't know what to think about it. But two or three times since then I have seen what seemed to be a ghost, and I know that as soon as the moment's past – you don't know what to think about it. I didn't know what to think about the little ivory fox either – the fox in my pocket. Who could have dropped it where I found it? One of our uncles long ago? Obviously, when a thing's dropped like that it doesn't vanish into the never never. It has to stay right there. So this fox could have been there long before our uncles. Long, long, long before. Like the stones. What made me feel slightly giddy was the way I'd found it while we were actually burying that fox. I did not know what to make of any of it. I could not see any way past it. When I thought about it, I felt a ring tightening round my head.

But there was the ivory fox in my pocket, so smooth and perfect. And after all these years, here it is, just as

I found it. And I still do not know what to make of it. Or of that old lady either. If it was an old lady.

Later that year we moved away to another part of Yorkshire. I did not walk up Crimsworth Dene again, to look at the fox's grave, for many, many years.

The Guitarist
Grace Hallworth

Joe was always in demand for the Singings, or community evenings held in villages which were too far away from the city to enjoy its attractions. He was an excellent guitarist and when he wasn't performing on his own, he accompanied the singers and dancers who also attended the Singing.

After a Singing someone was sure to offer Joe a lift back to his village but on one occasion he found himself stranded miles away from his home with no choice but to set out on foot. It was a dark night and there wasn't a soul to be seen on the road, not even a cat or a dog, so Joe began to strum his guitar to hearten himself for the lonely journey ahead.

Joe had heard many stories about strange things seen at night on that road but he told himself that most of the people who related these stories had been drinking heavily. All the same, as he came to a crossroad known to be the haunt of Lajables and other restless spirits, he strummed his guitar loudly to drown the rising clamour of fearful thoughts in his head. In the quiet of early morning the tune was sharp and strong, and Joe began to move to the rhythm; but all the while his eyes were fixed on a point ahead of him where four roads met. The nearer he got, the more convinced he was that someone was standing in the middle of the road. He hoped with all his heart that he was wrong and that the shape was only a shadow cast by an overhanging tree.

The man stood so still he might have been a statue, and it was only when Joe was within arm's length of the figure that he saw any sign of life. The man was quite tall, and so thin that his clothes hung on him as though they were thrown over a wire frame. There was a musty smell about them. It was too dark to see who the man was or what he looked like, and when he spoke his voice had a rasp to it which set Joe's teeth on edge.

'You play a real fine guitar for a youngster,' said the man, falling into step beside Joe.

Just a little while before, Joe would have given anything to meet another human being but somehow he was not keen to have this man as a companion. Nevertheless his motto was 'Better to be safe than sorry' so he was as polite as his unease would allow.

'It's nothing special, but I like to keep my hand in. What about you, man? Can you play guitar too?' asked Joe.

'Let me try your guitar and we'll see if I can match you,' replied the man. Joe handed over his guitar and the man began to play so gently and softly that Joe had to listen closely to hear the tune. He had never heard such a mournful air. But soon the music changed, the tune became wild and the rhythm fast and there was a harshness about it which drew a response from every nerve in Joe's body. Suddenly there was a new tone and mood and the music became light and enchanting. Joe felt as if he were borne in the air like a blown-up balloon. He was floating on a current of music and would follow it to the ends of the earth and beyond.

And then the music stopped. Joe came down to earth with a shock as he realized that he was standing in front of his house. The night clouds were slowly dispersing. The man handed the guitar back to Joe who was still dazed.

'Man, that was guitar music like I never heard in this world before,' said Joe.

'True.' said the man. 'You should have heard me when I was alive!'

The Servant

Alison Prince

Ginny ran down the path. Her mother shouted after her from the back door, 'When you've got a house of your own, my girl, you can make as much mess as you like. But you're not having your pocket money until you've tidied your bedroom!'

Ginny snatched her bike out of the shed, kicked the side gate open and set off down the lane. Her mother was waving her arms frantically and shouting something, but Ginny took no notice. Summer holidays were *awful*, she fumed, pedalling fast. Just because there was no school to go to, people treated you as if you were nothing at all – just a meek little figure who had to fit in with the rest of the household and not be noticed. A handy person to boss about. Run round to the shops, Ginny, dry the dishes, Ginny, tidy your room, Ginny. It was like being a *servant*.

Ginny came to the top of Bunkers Hill and let the bike freewheel down the long slope. The wind blew her hair back and made the hot morning cooler. Below her the green landscape spread out like a toy farmyard. Further down, Bunkers Hill crossed the busy main road and became Nebbutts Lane, leading through the distant fields to Cuckoo Wood where the bluebells grew so thickly in the spring. Much nearer, just before the crossroads, a disused track wandered off to the right. Ginny touched her brakes to check the bike's speed as she approached the junction. Nothing happened.

Panic clutched at Ginny's heart like a cold hand. The sunny day was whistling past her with a speed which made her eyes run. She grabbed repeatedly at the useless brakes, remembering now that she had told her father when he came home from work last night that they needed adjusting. The brakes had been slack yesterday, but now they had completely gone. And she was hurtling towards the busy highway. To go out there at this speed meant almost certain death.

There was only one escape. The track. A milk float was coming up the hill towards her, threatening to block the entry to Ginny's haven unless she got there first. She crouched over the handlebars to increase the bike's breakneck speed and banked the bike hard to her right. She missed the oncoming milk float by inches and caught a glimpse of the driver's startled face as she shot down the stony, disused lane.

The bicycle jumped and rattled over the rough surface but, to Ginny's relief, the track began to level out as it narrowed to an overgrown path between dark trees and straggling banks of brambles. Impeded by the long grass, the bike slowed down and at last stopped. Ginny got off shakily. Her knees and elbows felt as if they had turned to water.

After a few minutes she bent down and looked at the bike's brakes. They had been disconnected and the blocks removed. Her father must have been intending to buy some new ones for her today. But why hadn't he *said*? True, she had been out at a disco last night, but he could have left a note or told her mother . . . Ginny had an uneasy memory of her mother shouting something after her as she rode off this morning, but she thrust the thought away. Her parents simply didn't *care*, she told herself with a new burst of anger after being so frightened.

And now what? She had come out with every intention of staying out until lunchtime and she didn't want to go crawling home again so soon, no doubt to be bossed about and scolded for not stopping to listen to what her mother had been saying. Ginny propped the bike against the ivy-clad trunk of a tree and stared round her. It was very, very quiet. The trees seemed almost to meet overhead, shutting out the sunshine. Ginny gave a little shiver. And then she heard the bell.

It was a faint, tinkling bell, very distant. It rang with a peremptory rapidness as if shaken by an impatient hand. Somebody wanted something, and quickly. Ginny pushed her hands into her jeans pockets and set off along the path, leaving the bike where it was. Since she had nothing to do, she might as well go and find out where the sound of the bell had come from.

The path went on between its high banks in such deep shade that it was almost like being in a tunnel. Daylight glowed at its far end as if promising a clearing, and Ginny walked towards it quickly. The bell rang again, sounding closer this time. Ginny emerged from the trees to find that she had come out further along the hillside. The path ended in a field of ripening barley. Butterflies danced in the sun.

On the sloping ground beside the field, slate-roofed behind a flint wall with a gate in the middle, stood a house. Heavy lace curtains were tied in loops at its windows, and its doorstep was spotlessly white. A plume of smoke ascended from its chimney straight into the windless sky. As Ginny stared at the house, the bell sounded again, a longer, rattling tinkle. A looped curtain twitched back in the ground-floor window to the left of the front door and a face looked out. White hair, a high-necked blouse and two black eyes which stared accusingly.

'Violet! Come along in at once!' snapped a dry voice, and a finger tapped on the pane.

Ginny glanced over her shoulder in case somebody called Violet was standing behind her, but she was alone. The butterflies danced above the motionless barley.

The bell tinkled again, and this time Ginny's hand reached for the latch of the gate and she found herself running up the path. The untrodden whiteness of the front doorstep warned her not to enter this way, and she darted round the side of the house to where blue-flowered periwinkles fringed a paved yard. The back door stood open.

The large, dim kitchen had a red tiled floor, and a huge wooden plate rack stood above the stone sink like an ominous, complicated cage. Ginny found that she was listening intently, in a kind of dread. She was waiting for the bell to ring. In a few moments its jangling tinkle sounded, so close that it was almost inside her head. She ran through the shadowed hall, where patches of red and blue light gleamed from a panel of stained glass in the front door, and tapped on the white-painted door to her right.

'Come *in*,' said the dry voice impatiently.

Ginny opened the sitting-room door. The fingers which gripped the small brass bell by its ebony handle were thin and bony, the hand blue-veined, veiled by a ruffle of lace from the tight silk sleeve. Tiny jet buttons ran up the narrow bodice to the cameo at the high neck, and then there was the white face, the mouth thin and pinched and the nose as craggy as a parrot's beak, the eyes astonishingly black under the elaborate pile of white hair.

'You are not to go outside, Violet,' said the woman. 'You belong in here, with me.'

Ginny found that she was standing with her hands behind her and her feet together, and almost smiled at her own sudden politeness. 'My name's Ginny,' she said.

'Not suitable,' said the woman heavily. The black eyes travelled slowly down Ginny's figure until they reached her plimsolls, then travelled up again. Vertical lines appeared above the lips as the mouth tightened a little more.

'Violet,' said the woman, 'you will wear your uniform at all times in this house, do you understand?'

'But I'm not –' began Ginny. Her voice petered out as the tight lips smiled grimly.

'Oh, yes, you are, my dear,' said the woman. 'My servants have always been called Violet. So much more convenient. I am Mrs Rackham, but you will call me madam, of course.'

Ginny shook her head in confusion. This could not be happening. But she looked at the little brass bell with the ebony handle, and stared in Mrs Rackham's black, unblinking eyes, and knew that it was true.

'I have been *waiting* for my breakfast,' said Mrs Rackham.

Ginny stared guiltily into the black eyes, struggling to hold on to the idea that Mrs Rackham's breakfast had nothing to do with her, Ginny Thompson.

Mrs Rackham leaned forward a little. 'Light the spirit lamp,' she instructed impatiently, 'then go to the kitchen and get my breakfast.' The blue-veined hand gestured towards the table which stood by the window, draped with a lace cloth over heavy red chenille. On it stood eggshell-thin cups and saucers, a silver teapot and sugar bowl and a thin-spouted brass kettle which, supported on a brass stand, stood over a small burner. Ginny moved towards it. At any rate, she thought, it was better than hanging about at home. If she was treated like a servant there, she might just as well play at being a servant here.

A box of matches lay beside the brass kettle. Ginny struck one and turned up the wick in its holder. It burned with a steady blue flame. The old woman was mad, of course, Ginny told herself. It wasn't unusual in old people. Her own granny had been very absent-minded, always calling Ginny by the name of a long-dead aunt, Flora, which was even worse than Violet.

'That's better,' said Mrs Rackham, darting a black-eyed glance at the spirit lamp. 'Now get along to the kitchen, quickly. When you bring my breakfast, you will be properly dressed.'

Ginny smiled and said, 'All right.'

Mrs Rackham looked outraged. 'That is not the way to answer,' she snapped. 'Say, "yes, madam". And curtsy.'

Ginny held out imaginary skirts and curtsied deeply as she had been taught at her ballet class.

Mrs Rackham seemed even more angry. 'Just a small bob, you stupid creature!' she hissed. 'Do you girls know *nothing* these days?'

Ginny expected to feel amused as she gave an obedient little bob, but as Mrs Rackham growled

'That's better', and the black eyes bored into Ginny's mind, the hidden smile shrivelled and died.

Ginny left the room with quick, neat footsteps, closing the door quietly behind her. As she made her way back to the kitchen the voice of reason in her mind urged her to walk out of the door and back along the lane to her brakeless bicycle, and start pushing it home. On the other hand ... Mrs Rackham had to have her breakfast. Perhaps whoever looked after her had gone out for a while. No doubt they would be back.

The kitchen was cool and quiet. Greenish light filtered through a small, ivy-covered window, and a few flies circled aimlessly under the high ceiling. Gazing up at them, Ginny saw that a black dress and several white aprons hung from a wooden airer, and a starched white cap dangled from the end of one of its bars. She unhitched the airer's rope from its hook on the wall and released it hand over hand, lowering the airer to that she could reach the clothes. If she was going to humour the old lady's delusions, she might as well do the job properly.

But as Ginny peeled off her T-shirt and jeans she found that she was listening in a kind of terror for Mrs Rackham's bell; as if its demanding tinkle had dominated her whole life. She struggled into the black dress and did up the rows of buttons down the front and on each sleeve. She pulled on the thick black stockings which she also found on the airer, sliding up the pair of elastic garters which were looped round the airer's end beside the cap. Then she tied on a white, lace-edged apron and pulled the starched cap over her curly hair. She looked round for something more suitable than her plimsolls and found, neatly placed beside the wooden mangle, a pair of highly-polished black shoes, fastened by a single button.

The shoes fitted as if Ginny had always worn them. She pulled up the airer, then stared round the kitchen with increasing anxiety. What did madam have for breakfast? Plates of all sizes stood in the cage-like wooden plate rack, but there seemed to be no fridge and the pantry contained no muesli or cornflakes.

Mrs Rackham's bell rang.

Ginny jumped round, a hand to the high-buttoned neck of her dress. The voice of reason seemed to have deserted her, and she could only think that madam was waiting for her breakfast and that she, Violet, had failed to get it yet. She ran to the front room.

'Do I have to wait all day?' demanded Mrs Rackham. A vigorous spurt of steam was hissing from the brass kettle over its burner.

'I – I'm sorry, madam,' stammered Ginny. 'I didn't know what you wanted.'

'Two lightly boiled eggs, brown bread and butter cut in fingers, toast and marmalade,' said Mrs Rackham. 'Stupid girl. You can make the tea now you are here.'

Ginny went across to the table. She found an ornate tea caddy and put two spoonfuls of tea into the silver teapot. Then she picked up the brass kettle – and let it fall back into its stand with a gasp of pain. The handle was almost red hot. Tears sprang to Ginny's eyes as she nursed her stinging pain, but Mrs Rackham threw herself back in her chair, convulsed with cruel laughter. 'They all burn their hands!' she cackled delightedly. 'It's always the same – again and again!' Then, just as suddenly, she was angry. 'Turn the burner down, you idiot,' she snapped. 'The room is full of steam. And fetch a kettle holder.'

In the pale light of the kitchen, Ginny looked at her hand and saw the long red weal across the palm, and wanted to sit down and cry. But Mrs Rackham's bell was ringing, and she snatched the kettle holder from its hook beside the great black range and ran back to the sitting-room. She made the tea and said, 'I'll go and boil the eggs.'

'*When* you have moved the table within my reach,' said Mrs Rackham. 'And where is the milk?'

Ginny pushed the heavy table across to the old lady's chair, hampered by the stinging pain in her hand. Then she ran back to the kitchen for the milk, which she found by some kind of instinct in a small lidded churn on the pantry shelf. She snatched a blue jug from its hook and ladled some milk into it. The bell was ringing.

'That is a *kitchen* jug!' screamed Mrs Rackham as Ginny proffered the milk, and lace ruffles flew as a hand flashed out, sweeping the jug from Ginny's hand to smash against the sideboard. 'Clear all that mess up,' Mrs Rackham commanded, her face tight with fury, 'then bring my milk in the proper jug. Where are my eggs? Don't you dare boil them for more than three minutes!'

Ginny ran sobbing to the kitchen, found a small glass jug and filled it with milk then carried it back to Mrs Rackham, who said nothing. Milk dripped from the polished edge of the mahogany sideboard.

As Ginny went in search of a cloth she tried to recall the reasonable voice which told her that she did not belong here; but there was nothing in her mind except worry and guilt and the stinging of her burned hand. She found a rather smelly piece of rag and cleaned up the spilt milk as best she could, and picked up the pieces of the broken jug.

'Violet, *where* are my eggs?' enquired Mrs Rackham.

'Coming,' said Ginny desperately.

'Coming, *madam*!' shouted Mrs Rackham.

'Coming, madam,' Ginny repeated, and went out with a little curtsy, wiping her eyes on her sleeve. The bell tinkled and she turned back.

The black eyes were fixed upon her with a new energy as the tea was sipped, the cup returned with neat precision to its saucer. 'Have you done the fires?' asked Mrs Rackham. 'Black-leaded the grates, washed the hearths, swept the carpets, dusted? Cleaned the knives, whitened the doorstep, done the washing, scrubbed the kitchen floor? And what about the bedrooms? Are the beds clean and aired?'

'I don't know,' said Ginny helplessly. Tears overwhelmed her.

'I don't know, *madam*!' screamed Mrs Rackham.

Ginny fled to the safety of the kitchen, shaking. She found eggs in a large bowl, and an egg timer with red sand in the lower half of its double-bulged shape. She took a saucepan from the shelf, still crying a little, and filled it with hot water from the huge black kettle which steamed on the range.

Ginny found that her burned hand was beginning to blister. Like a remembered dream, a voice in her head told her that she did not have to stay here. There was a memory, too, of wearing different clothes. Trousers, a shirt made of soft stuff which left her arms bare . . . Ginny wiped her eyes on her black sleeve again, with a gesture so familiar that it seemed as if she had done it many times before. She gazed round the kitchen as if seeking those other garments, but the wooden chairs with a pattern of pierced holes in the seats were bare in the dim light, and the flies circled endlessly against the high ceiling.

The water in the saucepan began to bubble, and Ginny lowered in two eggs with a spoon, then turned over the egg timer. As the trickle of red sand began to run through the narrow neck, she got a brown loaf out of the earthenware bread crock and cut two slices, biting her lip because of the pain in her hand. Then she buttered the slices and cut them neatly into fingers.

When the eggs were done, she assembled a tray and carried it through the hall to Mrs Rackham. The sitting-room was dazzling after the dim kitchen, for sunlight poured in through the long window. Outside, the barley shimmered in the sun and butterflies danced. Tears suddenly brimmed again in Ginny's eyes. She would never be free to walk through the fields, to come so fast down a steep hill that her eyes ran, but not with tears.

'Don't stand there gawping, Violet,' said Mrs Rackham. 'Put the things down here.'

Ginny obediently slid the tray on to the lace cloth.

'Where is my toast?' demanded Mrs Rackham.

'I – I didn't know how to make it,' Ginny faltered. Remotely, she remembered making toast by putting slices of bread into little slits in the top of – of what? She shook her head, confused. She had always been here. She would never leave. She would die here.

'With a toasting fork, you stupid girl, in front of the range,' said Mrs Rackham. She decapitated an egg then added, 'The spirit lamp has gone out. Light it.'

Ginny held a burning match to the wick, but no flame sprang up.

'Refill it,' snapped Mrs Rackham, waving an irritable hand towards the corner cupboard.

Ginny opened the tall, panelled door and took out the bottle of spirit. Violet, she thought as she gazed at its wonderful purple colour. Violet. Like me.

With the kettle holder she gingerly removed the top of the burner and filled up its reservoir with spirit. Her burned hand made her clumsy and the spirit spilled over and ran down on to the lace cloth, soaking through into the red chenille below it. Ginny shot a fearful glance at Mrs Rackham, but madam was probing an egg with the delicate silver spoon, and did not look up. Ginny fed the wick carefully back into the reservoir and fitted the top into place again. Once more she struck a match and applied it to the wick.

A blue flame leapt up, not only from the wick but from the whole top of the burner, following the spilt spirit down the brass stand and on to the soaked cloth under it. Ginny shrieked with terror and jumped back, brushing against the uncorked bottle of spirit with her sleeve as she did so and knocking it over. More spirit gushed out, and sheets of flame sprang up, engulfing the kettle and its stand, the teapot, the cups, the table. Mrs Rackham began to scream, her mouth wide open in the white face, her blue-veined hands upraised. The red chenille cloth was ablaze, and the varnish on the heavy mahogany table legs was wrinkling as it caught fire. Flames began to leap up the side of the chintz arm chair where Mrs Rackham sat, still screaming. The skirt of her silk dress shrivelled as the flames licked across the chair, and Ginny saw that Mrs Rackham's legs were as twisted and useless as a rag doll's, encased in heavy contraptions of iron and leather.

Outside, the dancing butterflies shivered behind a screen of heat as the looped curtains burned. The room filled with smoke, and Ginny began to gasp for breath. Suddenly she realized that she must get out. She could not help Mrs Rackham. The hem of her long black dress was beginning to smoulder as she ran from the room. She grappled with the bolt on the front door. Her dress was burning. The house was full of fire, and the red and blue stained glass windows in the front door were dimmed with the choking smoke.

As Ginny wrenched the door open and daylight burst upon her like an explosion it seemed that Mrs Rackham was screaming a single word, senselessly and repeatedly.

'Again!' she shrieked, and it was like a mad song of agony and triumph. 'Again! Again! Again!' And Ginny knew what the terrible word meant. Like a recurring nightmare whose end only leads to the next beginning, she was condemned to repeat this experience over and over again. Even now, as the air fanned her burning dress into greedy flames and the screams were swallowed up in the inferno which had been a house; even in the agony of burning alive, Ginny was listening

Mrs Rackham's screams were swallowed up in the inferno

for the tinkle of Mrs Rackham's bell. It would all begin
again.

Somebody was shaking her. 'Ginny!' a voice was saying urgently. 'Are you all right? What are you doing
here?'

Mrs Thompson stared down at her daughter, who lay
huddled by the rusted gate in the flint wall, an arm
flung protectively across her face. She appeared to be
asleep.

'Again,' said Ginny, and trembled.

'Are you all right?' Mrs Thompson repeated. 'I was
frantic when you went off like that – your dad said to
tell you about the bike, that he'd get new brake blocks.
He'll murder me. Then the milkman said you nearly
crashed into him tearing down Bunkers Hill – well, I
got the car out straight away and came down here
looking for you.'

Ginny's eyes were open but she was not seeing her
mother. Her gaze searched the sky with a kind of
despair. 'Butterflies,' she murmured. Tears welled up
and she rubbed her eyes on the back of her wrist
wearily.

'Darling, don't cry,' said her mother. 'It's all right –
I'm not cross or anything. I mean, it was partly my
fault.' After a pause she went on, 'I found your bike
along the lane. But why did you come here? I hate
ruined houses, they're so creepy.' Rose bay willow
herb, the fire weed, stood tall among the blackened
heaps of stone. It really was a horrible place, Mrs
Thompson thought. Some distance away the
remains of a brass kettle lay dented and squashed in
the sun.

Ginny stood up and brushed fussily at her bare arms, fiddling at her wrists as though buttoning tight cuffs. Her mother watched with dawning concern as the girl straightened an apron, smoothed out a long skirt, her anxious hands not touching the surface of her jeans. 'I must go,' she said.

'You're not going anywhere,' said Ginny's mother. 'You're coming home with me. You must have had a nasty shock. We can put your bike in the back of the car.'

Ginny gave a sudden start. 'I must go,' she said again with worried alertness. 'Mrs Rackham wants her breakfast. That's her bell. What am I doing out here?'

Her mother stared. 'Mrs Rackham? This house is known as Rackham's, yes, but there's nobody here now. Some old crippled woman owned it, they say, but she died in the fire when it was burnt down, along with some poor little servant girl.'

'Violet,' agreed Ginny. She dropped a small curtsy, not looking at her mother, and called, 'Coming, madam!' Then she set off with oddly neat little foot-steps through the weed-grown rubble, trotting parallel to the garden wall until she turned at a right angle and ran on to where some blue-flowered periwinkle bloomed among the stone. Her mother intercepted her and caught the girl by the hand. Ginny flinched violently. A long, red, blistered weal lay across her palm.

'How on earth did you do that?' demanded her mother. 'There's nothing hot on a bicycle. Unless – you didn't put your hand on the tyre, did you, to try to stop?'

But Ginny did not hear. She was staring into the black eyes again, watching the thin mouth in the white face as the orders were snapped out, hearing the cruel laughter as she burned her hand again. Outside the tall window, the barley shimmered in the summer sun and the butterflies danced. But Ginny would never be free to walk among them again. She was Mrs Rackham's servant and madam wanted her breakfast. Again – and again – and again.

The Call

Robert Westall

I'm rota-secretary of our local Samaritans. My job's to see our office is staffed twenty-four hours a day, 365 days a year. It's a load of headaches, I can tell you. And the worst headache for any branch is overnight on Christmas Eve.

Christmas Night's easy; plenty have had enough of family junketings by then; nice to go on duty and give your stomach a rest. And New Year's Eve's OK, because we have Methodists and other teetotal types. But Christmas Eve . . .

Except we had Harry Lancaster.

In a way, Harry *was* the branch. Founder-member in 1963. A marvellous director all through the sixties. Available on the phone, day or night. Always the same quiet, unflappable voice, asking the right questions, soothing over-excited volunteers.

But he paid the price.

When he took early retirement from his firm in '73, we were glad. We thought we'd see even more of him. But we didn't. He took a six-month break from Sams. When he came back, he didn't take up the reins again. He took a much lighter job, treasurer. He didn't look ill, but he looked *faded*. Too long as a Sam. director can do that to you. But we were awfully glad just to have him back. No one was gladder than Maureen, the new director. Everybody cried on Maureen's shoulder, and Maureen cried on Harry's when it got rough.

Harry was the kind of guy you wish could go on for ever. But every so often, over the years, we'd realized he wasn't going to. His hair went snow-white; he got thinner and thinner. Gave up the treasurership. From doing a duty once a week, he dropped to once a month. But we still *had* him. His presence was everywhere in the branch. The new directors, leaders, he'd trained them all. They still asked themselves in a tight spot, 'What would Harry do?' And what he did do was as good as ever. But his birthday kept on coming round. People would say with horrified disbelief, 'Harry'll be *seventy-four* next year!'

And yet, most of the time, we still had in our minds the fifty-year-old Harry, full of life, brimming with new ideas. We couldn't do without that dark-haired ghost.

And the one thing he never gave up was overnight duty on Christmas Eve. Rain, hail or snow, he'd be there. Alone.

Now alone is wrong; the rules say the office must be double-staffed at all times. There are two emergency phones. How could even Harry cope with both at once?

But Christmas Eve is hell to cover. Everyone's got children or grandchildren, or is going away. And Harry had always done it alone. He said it was a quiet shift; hardly anybody ever rang. Harry's empty log-book was there to prove it; never more than a couple of long-term clients who only wanted to talk over old times and wish Harry Merry Christmas.

So I let it go on.

Until, two days before Christmas last year, Harry went down with flu. Bad. He tried dosing himself with all kinds of things; swore he was still coming. Was *desperate* to come. But Mrs Harry got in the doctor; and the doctor was adamant. Harry argued; tried getting out of bed and dressed to prove he was OK. Then he fell and cracked his head on the bedpost, and the doctor gave him a shot meant to put him right out. But Harry, raving by this time, kept trying to get up, saying he must go . . .

But I only heard about that later. As rota-secretary I had my own troubles, finding his replacement. The rule is that if the rota-bloke can't get a replacement, he does the duty himself. In our branch, anyway. But I was already doing the seven-to-ten shift that night, then driving north to my parents.

Eighteen fruitless phone calls later, I got somebody. Meg and Geoff Charlesworth. Just married; no kids.

When they came in at ten to relieve me, they were happy. Maybe they'd had a couple of drinks in the course of the evening. They were laughing; but they were certainly fit to drive. It is wrong to accuse them, as some did, later, of having had too many. Meg gave me a Christmas kiss. She'd wound a bit of silver tinsel through her hair, as some girls do at Christmas. They'd brought long red candles to light, and mince pies to heat up in our kitchen and eat at midnight. It was just happiness; and it *was* Christmas Eve.

Then my wife tooted our car horn outside, and I passed out of the story. The rest is hearsay; from the log they kept, and the reports they wrote, that were still lying in the in-tray the following morning.

They heard the distant bells of the parish church, filtering through the falling snow, announcing midnight. Meg got the mince pies out of the oven, and Geoff was just kissing her, mouth full of flaky pastry, when the emergency phone went.

Being young and keen, they both grabbed for it. Meg won. Geoff shook his fist at her silently, and dutifully logged the call. Midnight exactly, according to his new watch. He heard Meg say what she'd been carefully coached to say, like Samaritans the world over.

'Samaritans – can I help you?'

She said it just right. Warm, but not gushing. Interested, but not *too* interested. That first phrase is all-important. Say it wrong, the client rings off without speaking.

Meg frowned. She said the phrase again. Geoff crouched close in support, trying to catch what he could from Meg's ear-piece. He said afterwards the line was very bad. Crackly, very crackly. Nothing but crackles, coming and going.

Meg said her phrase the third time. She gestured to Geoff that she wanted a chair. He silently got one, pushed it in behind her knees. She began to wind her fingers into the coiled telephone cord, like all Samaritans do when they're anxious.

Meg said into the phone, 'I'd like to help if I can.' It was good to vary the phrase, otherwise clients began to think you were a tape recording. She added, 'My name's Meg. What can I call *you*?' You never ask for their *real* name, at that stage; always what you can call them. Often they start off by giving a false name . . .

A voice spoke through the crackle. A female voice.

'He's going to kill me. I know he's going to kill me.

137

When he comes back.' Geoff, who caught it from a distance, said it wasn't the phrases that were so awful. It was the way they were said.

Cold; so cold. And certain. It left no doubt in your mind he *would* come back and kill her. It wasn't a wild voice you could hope to calm down. It wasn't a cunning hysterical voice, trying to upset you. It wasn't the voice of a hoaxer, that to the trained Samaritan ear always has that little wobble in it, that might break down into a giggle at any minute and yet, till it does, must be taken absolutely seriously. Geoff said it was a voice as cold, as real, as hopeless as a tombstone.

'Why do you think he's going to kill you?' Geoff said Meg's voice was shaking, but only a little. Still warm, still interested.

Silence. Crackle.

'Has he threatened you?'

When the voice came again, it wasn't an answer to her question. It was another chunk of lonely hell, being spat out automatically; as if the woman at the other end was really only talking to herself.

'He's gone to let a boat through the lock. When he comes back, he's going to kill me.'

Meg's voice tried to go up an octave; she caught it just in time.

'Has he *threatened* you? What is he going to do?'

'He's goin' to push me in the river, so it looks like an accident.'

'Can't you swim?'

'There's half an inch of ice on the water. Nobody could live a minute.'

'Can't you get away . . . before he comes back?'

'Nobody lives within miles. And I'm lame.'

'Can't I . . . you . . . ring the police?'

Geoff heard a click, as the line went dead. The dialling tone resumed. Meg put the phone down wearily, and suddenly shivered, though the office was over-warm, from the roaring gas fire.

'I'm so *cold*!'

Geoff brought her cardigan, and put it round her. 'Shall I ring the duty-director, or will you?'

'You. If you heard it all.'

Tom Brett came down the line, brisk and cheerful. 'I've not gone to bed yet. Been filling the little blighter's Christmas stocking . . .'

Geoff gave him the details. Tom Brett was everything a good duty-director should be. Listened without interrupting; came back solid and reassuring as a house.

'Boats don't go through the locks this time of night. Haven't done for twenty years. The old alkali steamers used to, when the alkali trade was still going strong. The locks are only manned nine till five nowadays. Pleasure boats can wait till morning. As if anyone would be moving a pleasure boat this weather . . .'

'Are you *sure*?' asked Geoff doubtfully.

'Quite sure. Tell you something else – the river's nowhere near freezing over. Runs past my back fence. Been watching it all day, 'cos I bought the lad a fishing rod for Christmas, and it's not much fun if he can't try it out. You've been *had*, old son. Some Christmas joker having you on. Goodnight!'

'Hoax call,' said Geoff heavily, putting the phone down. 'No boats going through locks. No ice on the river. Look!' He pulled back the curtain from the office

139

window. 'It's still quite warm out – the snow's melting, not even lying.'

Meg looked at the black wet road, and shivered again. 'That was no hoax. Did you think that voice was a hoax?'

'We'll do what the boss-man says. Ours not to reason why . . .'

He was still waiting for the kettle to boil, when the emergency phone went again.

The same voice.

'But he *can't* just push you in the river and get away with it!' said Meg desperately.

'He can. I always take the dog for a walk last thing. And there's places where the bank is crumbling and the fence's rotting. And the fog's coming down. He'll break a bit of fence, then put the leash on the dog, and throw it in after me. Doesn't matter whether the dog drowns or is found wanderin'. Either'll suit *him*. Then he'll ring the police an' say I'm missin' . . .'

'But why should he *want* to? What've you *done*? To deserve it?'

'I'm gettin' old. I've got a bad leg. I'm not much use to him. He's got a new bit o' skirt down the village . . .'

'But can't we . . .'

'All you can do for me, love, is to keep me company till he comes. It's lonely . . . That's not much to ask, is it?'

'Where *are* you?'

Geoff heard the line go dead again. He thought Meg looked like a corpse herself. White as a sheet. Dull dead eyes, full of pain. Ugly, almost. How she would look as an old woman, if life was rough on her. He hovered, helpless, desperate, while the whistling kettle wailed from the warm Samaritan kitchen.

'Ring Tom again, for goodness sake,' said Meg, savagely.

Tom's voice was a little less genial. He'd got into bed and turned the light off . . .

'Same joker, eh? Bloody persistent. But she's getting her facts wrong. No fog where I am. Any where you are?'

'No,' said Geoff, pulling back the curtain again, feeling a nitwit.

'There were no fog warnings on the late-night weather forecast. Not even for low-lying districts . . .'

'No.'

'Well, I'll try to get my head down again. But don't hesitate to ring if anything *serious* crops up. As for this other lady . . . if she comes on again, just try to humour her. Don't argue – just try to make a relationship.'

In other words, thought Geoff miserably, don't bother me with *her* again.

But he turned back to a Meg still frantic with worry. Who would not be convinced. Even after she'd rung the local British Telecom weather summary, and was told quite clearly the night would be clear all over the Eastern Region.

'I want to know where she *is*. I want to know where she's ringing from . . .'

To placate her, Geoff got out the large-scale Ordnance Survey maps that some offices carry. It wasn't a great problem. The Ousam was a rarity; the only canalized river with locks for fifty miles around. And there were only eight sets of locks on it.

'These four,' said Geoff, 'are right in the middle of towns and villages. So it can't be *them*. And there's a whole row of Navigation cottages at Sutton's Lock, and I know they're occupied, so it can't be *there*. And this last one – Ousby Point – is right on the sea and it's all docks and stone quays – there's no river-bank to crumble. So it's either Yaxton Bridge, or Moresby Abbey locks . . .'

The emergency phone rang again. There is a myth among old Samaritans that you can tell the quality of the incoming call by the sound of the phone bell. Sometimes it's lonely, sometimes cheerful, sometimes downright frantic. Nonsense, of course. A bell is a bell is a bell . . .

But this ringing sounded so cold, so dreary, so dead, that for a second they both hesitated and looked at each other with dread. Then Meg slowly picked the phone up; like a bather hesitating on the bank of a cold grey river.

It was the voice again.

'The boat's gone through. He's just closing the lock gates. He'll be here in a minute . . .'

'What kind of boat is it?' asked Meg, with a desperate attempt at self-defence.

The voice sounded put out for a second, then said, 'Oh, the usual. One of the big steamers. The *Lowestoft*, I think. Aye, the lock gates are closed. He's coming up the path. Stay with me, love. Stay with me . . .'

Geoff took one look at his wife's grey, frozen, horrified face, and snatched the phone from her hand. He might be a Samaritan; but he was a husband, too. He wasn't sitting and watching his wife being messed around by some vicious hoaxer.

'Now *look*!' he said. 'Whoever you are! We want to help. We'd like to help. But stop feeding us lies. I know the *Lowestoft*. I've been aboard her. They gave her to the Sea Scouts, for a headquarters. She hasn't got an engine any more. She's a hulk. She's never moved for years. Now let's cut the cackle . . .'

The line went dead.

'Oh, *Geoff*!' said Meg.

'Sorry. But the moment I called her bluff, she rang off. That *proves* she's a hoaxer. All those old steamers were broken up for scrap, except the *Lowestoft*. She's a *hoaxer*, I tell you!'

'Or an old lady who's living in the past. Some old lady who's muddled and lonely and frightened. And you shouted at her . . .'

He felt like a murderer. It showed in his face. And she made the most of it.

'Go out and find her, Geoff. Drive over and see if you can find her . . .'

'And leave you alone in the office? Tom'd have my guts for garters . . .'

'Harry Lancaster always did it alone. I'll lock the door. I'll be all right. Go on, Geoff. She's lonely. Terrified.'

He'd never been so torn in his life. Between being a husband and being a Samaritan. That's why a lot of branches won't let husband and wife do duty together. We won't, now. We had a meeting about it; afterwards.

'Go *on*, Geoff. If she does anything silly, I'll never forgive myself. She might chuck herself in the river . . .'

They both knew. In our parts, the river or the drain is often the favourite way; rather than the usual overdose. The river seems to *call* to the locals, when life gets too much for them.

'Let's ring Tom again . . .'

She gave him a look that withered him and Tom together. In the silence that followed, they realized they were cut off from their duty-director, from *all* the directors, from *all* help. The most fatal thing, for Samaritans. They were poised on the verge of the ultimate sin; going it alone.

He made a despairing noise in his throat; reached for his coat and the car keys. 'I'll do Yaxton Bridge. But I'll not do Moresby Abbey. It's a mile along the towpath in the dark. It'd take me an hour . . .'

He didn't wait for her dissent. He heard her lock the office door behind him. At least she'd be safe behind a locked door . . .

He never thought that telephones got past locked doors.

He made Yaxton Bridge in eight minutes flat, skidding and correcting his skids on the treacherous road. Lucky there wasn't much traffic about.

On his right, the River Ousam beckoned, flat, black, deep and still. A slight steam hung over the water, because it was just a little warmer than the air.

It was getting on for one, by the time he reached the lock. But there was still a light in one of the pair of lock-keeper's cottages. And he knew at a glance that this wasn't the place. No ice on the river; no fog. He hovered, unwilling to disturb the occupants. Maybe they were in bed, the light left on to discourage burglars.

But when he crept up the garden path, he heard the sound of the TV, a laugh, coughing. He knocked.

An elderly man's voice called through the door, 'Who's there?'

'Samaritans. I'm trying to find somebody's house. I'll push my card through your letter-box.'

He scrabbled frantically through his wallet in the dark. The door was opened. He passed through to a snug sitting room, a roaring fire. The old man turned down the sound of the TV. The wife said he looked perished, and the Samaritans did such good work, turning out at all hours, even at Christmas. Then she went to make a cup of tea.

He asked the old man about ice, and fog, and a lock-keeper who lived alone with a lame wife. The old man shook his head. 'Couple who live next door's got three young kids . . .'

'Wife's not lame, is she?'

'Nay – a fine-lookin' lass wi' two grand legs on her . . .'

His wife, returning with the tea tray, gave him a *very* old-fashioned look. Then she said, 'I've sort of got a memory of a lock-keeper wi' a lame wife – this was years ago, mind. Something not nice . . . but your memory goes, when you get old.'

'We worked the lock at Ousby Point on the coast, all our married lives,' said the old man apologetically. 'They just let us retire here, 'cos the cottage was goin' empty . . .'

Geoff scalded his mouth, drinking their tea, he was so frantic to get back. He did the journey in seven minutes; he was getting used to the skidding, by that time.

* * *

He parked the car outside the Sam. office, expecting her to hear his return and look out. But she didn't.

He knocked; he shouted to her through the door. No answer. Frantically he groped for his own key in the dark, and burst in.

She was sitting at the emergency phone, her face greyer than ever. Her eyes were far away, staring at the blank wall. They didn't swivel to greet him. He bent close to the phone in her hand and heard the same voice, the same cold hopeless tone, going on and on. It was sort of . . . hypnotic. He had to tear himself away, and grab a message pad. On it he scrawled, 'WHAT'S HAPPENING? WHERE IS SHE?'

He shoved it under Meg's nose. She didn't respond in any way at all. She seemed frozen, just listening. He pushed her shoulder, half angry, half frantic. But she was wooden, like a statue. Almost as if she was in a trance. In a wave of husbandly terror, he snatched the phone from her.

It immediately went dead.

He put it down, and shook Meg. For a moment she recognized him and smiled, sleepily. Then her face went rigid with fear.

'Her husband was in the house. He was just about to open the door where she was . . .'

'Did you find out where she was?'

'Moresby Abbey lock. She told me in the end. I got her confidence. Then *you* came and ruined it . . .'

She said it as if he was suddenly her enemy. An enemy, a fool, a bully, a murderer. Like all men. Then she said, 'I must go to her . . .'

'And leave the office unattended? That's *mad*.' He took off his coat with the car keys, and hung it on the office door. He came back and looked at her again. She still seemed a bit odd, trance-like. But she smiled at him and said, 'Make me a quick cup of tea. I must go to the loo, before she rings again.'

Glad they were friends again, he went and put the kettle on. Stood impatiently waiting for it to boil, tapping his fingers on the sink unit, trying to work out what they should do. He heard Meg's step in the hallway. Heard the toilet flush.

Then he heard a car start up outside.

His car.

He rushed out into the hall. The front door was swinging, letting in the snow. Where his car had been, there were only tyre marks.

He was terrified now. Not for the woman. For Meg.

He rang Tom Brett, more frightened than any client Tom Brett had ever heard.

He told Tom what he knew.

'Moresby Locks,' said Tom. 'A lame woman. A murdering husband. Oh no. I'll be with you in five.'

'The exchange are putting emergency calls through to Jimmy Henry,' said Tom, peering through the whirling wet flakes that were clogging his windscreen wipers. 'Do you know what way Meg was getting to Moresby Locks?'

'The only way,' said Geoff. 'Park at Wylop Bridge and walk a mile up the towpath.'

'There's a short cut. Down through the woods by the Abbey, and over the lock-gates. Not a lot of people know about it. I think we'll take that one. I want to get there before she does . . .'

'What the hell do you think's going on?'

147

'I've got an *idea*. But if I told you, you'd think I was out of my tiny shiny. So I won't. All I want is your Meg safe and dry, back in the Sam. office. And nothing in the log that headquarters might see . . .'

He turned off the by-pass, into a narrow track where hawthorn bushes reached out thorny arms and scraped at the paintwork of the car. After a long while, he grunted with satisfaction, clapped on the brakes and said, 'Come on.'

They ran across the narrow wooden walkway that sat precariously on top of the lock-gates. The flakes of snow whirled at them, in the light of Tom's torch. Behind the gates, the water stacked up, black, smooth, slightly steaming because it was warmer than the air. In an evil way, it called to Geoff. So easy to slip in, let the icy arms embrace you, slip away . . .

Then they were over, on the towpath. They looked left, right, listened.

Footsteps, woman's footsteps, to the right. They ran that way.

Geoff saw Meg's walking back, in its white raincoat . . .

And beyond Meg, leading Meg, another back, another woman's back. The back of a woman who limped.

A woman with a dog. A little white dog . . .

For some reason, neither of them called out to Meg. Fear of disturbing a Samaritan relationship, perhaps. Fear of breaking up something that neither of them understood. After all, they could afford to be patient now. They had found Meg safe. They were closing up quietly on her, only ten yards away. No danger . . .

Geoff saw Meg's walking back, in its white raincoat

Then, in the light of Tom's torch, a break in the white-painted fence on the river side.

And the figure of the limping woman turned through the gap in the fence, and walked out over the still black waters of the river.

And like a sleepwalker, Meg turned to follow . . .

They caught her on the very brink. Each of them caught her violently by one arm, like policemen arresting a criminal. Tom cursed, as one of his feet slipped down the bank and into the water. But he held on to them, as they all swayed on the brink, and he only got one very wet foot.

'What the hell am I doing here?' asked Meg, as if waking from a dream. 'She was talking to me. I'd got her confidence . . .'

'Did she tell you her name?'

'Agnes Todd.'

'Well,' said Tom, 'here's where Agnes Todd used to live.'

There were only low walls of stone, in the shape of a house. With stretches of concrete and old broken tile in between. There had been a phone, because there was still a telegraph pole, with a broken junction-box from which two black wires flapped like flags in the wind.

'Twenty-one years ago, Reg Todd kept this lock. His lame wife Agnes lived with him. They didn't get on well – people passing the cottage heard them quarrelling. Christmas Eve, 1964, he reported her missing to the police. She'd gone out for a walk with the dog, and not come back. The police searched. There was a bad fog down that night. They found a hole in the railing, just about where we saw one; and a hole in the ice, just glazing over. They found the dog's body next day; but they didn't find her for a month, till the ice on the River Ousam finally broke up.

'The police tried to make a case of it. Reg Todd *had* been carrying on with a girl in the village. But there were no marks of violence. In the end, she could have fallen, she could've been pushed, or she could've jumped. So they let Reg Todd go; and he left the district.'

There was a long silence. Then Geoff said, 'So you think . . .?'

'I think nowt,' said Tom Brett, suddenly very stubborn and solid and Fenman. 'I think nowt, and that's all I *know*. Now let's get your missus home.'

Nearly a year passed. In the November, after a short illness, Harry Lancaster died peacefully in his sleep. He had an enormous funeral. The church was full. Present Samaritans, past Samaritans from all over the country, more old clients than you could count, and even two of the top brass from Slough.

But it was not till everybody was leaving the house that Tom Brett stopped Geoff and Meg by the gate. More solid and Fenman than ever.

'I had a long chat wi' Harry,' he said, 'after he knew he was goin'. He told me. About Agnes Todd. She had rung him up on Christmas Eve. Every Christmas Eve for twenty years . . .'

'Did he know she was a . . .?' Geoff still couldn't say it.

'Oh, aye. No flies on Harry. The second year – while he was still director – he persuaded the GPO to get an engineer to trace the number. How he managed to get

151

them to do it on Christmas Eve, goodness only knows.
But he had a way with him, Harry, in his day.'

'And . . .'

'The GPO were baffled. It was the old number of the
lock-cottage all right. But the lock-cottage was
demolished a year after the . . . whatever it was. Nobody
would live there, afterwards. All the GPO found was a
broken junction-box and wires trailin'. Just like we saw
that night.'

'So he talked to her all those years . . . knowing?'

'Aye, but he wouldn't let anybody else do Christmas
Eve. She was lonely, but he knew she was dangerous.
Lonely an' dangerous. She wanted company.'

Meg shuddered. 'How could he bear it?'

'He was a Samaritan . . .'

'Why didn't he tell anybody?'

'Who'd have believed him?'

There were half a dozen of us in the office this Christmas Eve. Tom Brett, Maureen, Meg and Geoff, and me.
All waiting for . . .

It never came. Nobody called at all.

'Do you think . . .?' asked Maureen, with an attempt
at a smile, her hand to her throat in a nervous gesture,
in the weak light of dawn.

'Aye,' said Tom Brett. 'I think we've heard the last of
her. Mebbe Harry took her with him. Or came back for
her. Harry was like that. The best Samaritan I ever
knew.'

His voice went funny on the last two words, and
there was a shine on those stolid Fenman eyes. He said,
'I'll be off then.' And was gone.

ALSO IN

HEINEMANN
NEW WINDMILLS

Founding Editors: Anne and Ian Serraillier

Chinua Achebe Things Fall Apart
Vivien Alcock The Cuckoo Sister; The Monster Garden;
The Trial of Anna Cotman; A Kind of Thief; Ghostly Companions
Margaret Atwood The Handmaid's Tale
Jane Austen Pride and Prejudice
J G Ballard Empire of the Sun
Nina Bawden The Witch's Daughter; A Handful of Thieves; Carrie's
War; The Robbers; Devil by the Sea; Kept in the Dark; The Finding;
Keeping Henry; Humbug; The Outside Child
Valerie Bierman No More School
Melvin Burgess An Angel for May
Ray Bradbury The Golden Apples of the Sun; The Illustrated Man
Betsy Byars The Midnight Fox; Goodbye, Chicken Little; The
Pinballs; The Not-Just-Anybody Family; The Eighteenth Emergency
Victor Canning The Runaways; Flight of the Grey Goose
Ann Coburn Welcome to the Real World
Hannah Cole Bring in the Spring
Jane Leslie Conly Racso and the Rats of NIMH
Robert Cormier We All Fall Down; Tunes for Bears to Dance to
Roald Dahl Danny, The Champion of the World; The Wonderful
Story of Henry Sugar; George's Marvellous Medicine; The BFG;
The Witches; Boy; Going Solo; Matilda
Anita Desai The Village by the Sea
Charles Dickens A Christmas Carol; Great Expectations;
Hard Times; Oliver Twist; A Charles Dickens Selection
Peter Dickinson Merlin Dreams
Berlie Doherty Granny was a Buffer Girl; Street Child
Roddy Doyle Paddy Clarke Ha Ha Ha
Gerald Durrell My Family and Other Animals
Anne Fine The Granny Project
Anne Frank The Diary of Anne Frank
Leon Garfield Six Apprentices; Six Shakespeare Stories;
Six More Shakespeare Stories
Jamila Gavin The Wheel of Surya
Adele Geras Snapshots of Paradise

Alan Gibbons Chicken

Graham Greene The Third Man and The Fallen Idol; Brighton Rock

Thomas Hardy The Withered Arm and Other Wessex Tales

L P Hartley The Go-Between

Ernest Hemmingway The Old Man and the Sea; A Farewell to Arms

Nigel Hinton Getting Free; Buddy; Buddy's Song

Anne Holm I Am David

Janni Howker Badger on the Barge; Isaac Campion; Martin Farrell

Jennifer Johnston Shadows on Our Skin

Toeckey Jones Go Well, Stay Well

Geraldine Kaye Comfort Herself; A Breath of Fresh Air

Clive King Me and My Million

Dick King-Smith The Sheep-Pig

Daniel Keyes Flowers for Algernon

Elizabeth Laird Red Sky in the Morning; Kiss the Dust

D H Lawrence The Fox and The Virgin and the Gypsy;
Selected Tales

Harper Lee To Kill a Mockingbird

Ursula Le Guin A Wizard of Earthsea

Julius Lester Basketball Game

C Day Lewis The Otterbury Incident

David Line Run for Your Life

Joan Lingard Across the Barricades; Into Exile; The Clearance;
The File on Fraulein Berg

Robin Lister The Odyssey

Penelope Lively The Ghost of Thomas Kempe

Jack London The Call of the Wild; White Fang

Bernard Mac Laverty Cal; The Best of Bernard Mac Laverty

Margaret Mahy The Haunting

Jan Mark Do You Read Me? (Eight Short Stories)

James Vance Marshall Walkabout

W Somerset Maugham The Kite and Other Stories

Ian McEwan The Daydreamer; A Child in Time

Pat Moon The Spying Game

Michael Morpurgo Waiting for Anya; My Friend Walter;
The War of Jenkins' Ear

Bill Naughton The Goalkeeper's Revenge

New Windmill A Charles Dickens Selection

New Windmill Book of Classic Short Stories

New Windmill Book of Nineteenth Century Short Stories

How many have you read?